The Voice of the Wooden Dragon

The Voice of the Wooden Dragon

by
Christie Waldman

illustrated by
Lane Waldman

based on the notebooks of
Marcus A. Dragon

NFB Publishing
Buffalo, New York

NFB Publishing
119 Dorchester Road
Buffalo, New York 14213
For more information visit Nfbpublishing.com

To dragons and humans alike.
Especially two humans, Sasha and Charlie.

CONTENTS

PART THREE: JOURNEYS

"Say, has anyone seen my notebooks? They were here in my treasure chest a minute ago."
—Marcus Antigonus Dragon

Hold On A Minute!

Hi, Marcus A. Dragon here. Am I too late? (huff, huff). I got here as fast as I could—all the way from Deweydaire. I thought maybe you could help me. I just got word that someone named "Christie Waldman" has written a book based on my secret notebooks. Boy, am I mad at her! What I can't understand is how she got hold of them. You didn't give them to her, did you? No, I didn't think so.

What, the book has already been published? You're reading it right now! You're kidding, right? You're not kidding? *Sigh!*

You see, it's not easy being a dragon. Most people don't take us dragons seriously. Why, I've even had people say they could see right through me. Heh heh.

Say, you believe in me, don't you? Good. Just checking.

Beep! Someone's trying to reach me. It's Christie! Just a second.

Christie Waldman, I am M-A-D mad at you! How did you get hold of my notebooks! ... No, I won't listen! ... What's that? You say I'm your favorite author? Why, thank you! Now, wait a minute! Don't you try to flatter me! ... What's that, Christie? You think we should tell the story together? You can't be serious! ... Yes, I realize my options are limited .... You say you'll make me a co-author .... and you promise to let me have the last word .... Hmm....

I may regret this ..., but ..., okay, Christie. Let's tell the story to-

gether! But first, I'd like to say a few words to the readers, by way of introduction. You don't mind, do you?

* * *

Hi, it's me again, Marcus A. Dragon, co-author of *The Voice of the Wooden Dragon*. It's a story near and dear to my heart. It's about dragons and humans I once knew in Deweydaire. You've heard of Deweydaire, haven't you? You *haven't*? Come to think of it, why should you have? It's a faraway land ruled by dragons—who just happen to be vegetarians. We are *anthropomorphic*. In other words, we behave quite a bit like people, though we look and act like dragons. For the most part, we are civilized, though we've been known to revert to reptilian behavior, especially when stressed. Deweydaire is my home, though you will not find it on any map.

Almira Palace, in the land of Deweydaire, is a rustic stone castle built high up on a craggy cliff that overlooks a snarly sea, where waves crash upon rocks constantly. In the distance, if it's not too misty, one could just barely make out the foothills to the forbidding Deweydaire Mountains. On the border of Almira lay the neighboring kingdom of Guldavia. Unlike Guldavia, Almira was ruled by a queen (a dragon, of course). Which queen, you ask? Why, none other than that feisty old Queen Esmerelda— but you wouldn't want to hear about *her*, would you? You *would*? Hmm. Let me think about this …. You know, that's not a bad place to start!

The Authors

PART ONE:
A ROYAL MESS

CHAPTER ONE

Esmerelda the Enigma

It was a lovely morning in May. Dr. George Fitzhugh, that good dragon doctor, had a spring in his step as he bounded up the steps to his office inside Almira Palace, cup of "morning brew" in hand. Although there had been trouble with the queen lately, he felt confident that today would be different. Today he felt optimistic. Why, anything could happen today!

As usual, he wore his white lab coat over his green scaly body. A metal stethoscope hung around his neck. He had just sat down at his desk to "tuck into" some paperwork when he heard the familiar voice of his head nurse, calling him over the office intercom they had rigged up.

"Dr. Fitzhugh! Dr. Fitzhugh! Please come to the queen's bedchamber at once!"

Oh no! Not the queen again! What could it be this time? Grabbing his clipboard from his desk, Dr. Fitzhugh hastened down the hall to the queen's bedchamber, his talons clicking staccato against the cold stone floor. He reached her room just in time to see her flinging all her medicine bottles from her nightstand to the floor with one fell swoop of her frail-*looking* wing.

"Now look what you've done!" said the dragon doctor, taking a giant step towards his patient to avoid stepping in the mess of broken glass and oozing, sticky liquids.

"Go away," said the cranky queen, disappearing under the covers—all but her scaly dragon feet.

"All right," the doctor said briskly, taking charge. "Let's go through the usual tests, shall we? Are you strong enough to hold a pencil today?" He handed her a short, stubby yellow one.

The queen's green, taloned claw emerged from under the blankets, grabbed the pencil from the doctor, and threw it hard against the wall. "I'm tired of all these tests!" she said.

"Now look what you've done. You've made another mark on the wall," said the doctor. "We've just finished cleaning off all the marks you made last week."

"I'm the queen. I can do whatever I want. Get lost, buddy," snapped the queen.

"That is not how one speaks to the Chief Palace Physician," said the doctor, straightening his lab coat with dignity. "I'm your doctor, George Fitzhugh. Remember?"

"Fitz-*who*? Get out right now or I'll—"

Dr. Fitzhugh ducked as she threw a pillow at him. Then she picked up a vase full of flowers, as if to throw that at him, too.

"As you wish, Your Majesty," he said, making a very quick half-bow as he darted out the door. He shut it quickly, wincing at the sound of a vase smashing against the door.

"Whew!" he said to his head nurse when he was safely on the other side. "Whatever is making her act like this? She didn't even recognize me! I've tried every treatment in the book. I've consulted every specialist for miles around, but no one has a clue. I'm at my wit's end."

"There's one doctor you haven't consulted yet: Dr. Fred Samson," said his nurse.

"That wacky dragon doctor who lives way out in Newtesia!" exclaimed Dr. Fitzhugh. "There's a reason for that. You never know what *he* might suggest .... On the other hand, we've tried everything else. Do you really think I should call him?"

"He may be your last resort," said the nurse, being practical.

"I suppose you're right," Dr. Fitzhugh said with a sigh. He strode to his office to make the fateful call.

If Dr. Fitzhugh could have seen Dr. Samson just then, he might not have done so. Underneath his short white lab coat, Dr. Samson was wearing a green-and-black striped tee-shirt that matched his green scales. His shoes were a cross between sandals and sneakers, with openings for his talons. He had designed them himself. He was elated to be getting a phone call.

"Samson's Alternative Medicine!" Dr. Samson scooted his wheeled office chair over to his wall calendar to check off his first call of the week.

"Uh, I think I have the wrong number," said Dr. Fitzhugh.

"George Fitzhugh, is that you? How's my old golf buddy?" He began doodling on his notepad, drawing a caricature of Dr. Fitzhugh as a rather pear-shaped dragon with glasses sliding down his nose.

"Who has time for golf!" cried Dr. Fitzhugh (pushing up his glasses). "I've been worried sick about a certain patient of mine—none other than Queen Esmerelda herself."

"Oh?" Dr. Samson stopped his doodling abruptly. "What seems to be the problem, George?"

"I don't rightly know. Half of the time, she's moaning and groaning, Ai, *ai*, over and over again, like she's in great pain. But when I ask her what's wrong, she won't tell me. Also, she claims—or pretends, maybe—to be too weak to get out of bed.

"The other half of the time, though, you'd better watch out, for she can be very cantankerous. I found that out when I tried to take her teddy bear away from her."

"*You tried to take her teddy bear away from her?*" repeated Dr. Samson in disbelief. "Why would you do a thing like that, George? Forgive me, but—was that really necessary?"

"It needed washing—forget the teddy bear, George! We've got a serious situation on our hands. The country needs a strong ruler. We've got to get the queen up out of bed and back on her throne!"

"Yes, I see," said Dr. Samson, stroking the scales on his chin thoughtfully. "Obviously, this is a complicated case. There could be more going on here than 'meets the eye of newt,' so to speak—heh heh. Tell me, have you ever considered hypnosis? Perhaps the problem is *psychosomatic.*"

"You mean *all in her head*? I don't think so, Fred. The queen's ailment is real, even if we don't understand it."

"I don't doubt that, my friend, but the mind is complicated and can affect the body. Perhaps hypnosis would give us a clue into what is ailing your queen." Dr. Samson tilted back in his swivel office chair and toyed with his pencil.

"I don't know, Fred," said Dr. Fitzhugh, worried. "Don't you have any suggestions that aren't so risky?"

"Relax, George! Hypnosis is perfectly safe!"

Dr. Fitzhugh was hesitant. "I suppose we could try it, so long as you're *sure* it won't endanger the queen's life. How soon can you arrange for a hypnotist to come to the palace?"

"Let me see .... How about tomorrow around ten? I've just had a cancellation," said Dr. Samson.

"You! Since when are you a registered hypnotist?"

"Uh ... since yesterday—but don't worry; I know all the techniques," said Dr. Samson, eyeing with pride his diploma, framed and hanging on the wall, although the ink was barely dry. It's a good thing Dr. Fitzhugh could not see it, for it said, "Fred Samson, Apprentice Hypnotist, Newtesia Self-Study School of Hypnosis."

"Fred—"

"—Now, George, relax! I'll see you tomorrow around ten. In the meantime, why don't you give the queen a break from all those pencil tests? Ta-ta!!" *Click.*

CHAPTER TWO

A Doctor and
his Methods

Shortly after ten o'clock the next morning, Dr. Fitzhugh and two of his most trusted dragon nurses were gathered at the queen's bedside. Dr. Fitzhugh had begun tapping his talons expectantly when Dr. Samson finally breezed in at ten thirty, wearing a T-shirt that had a necktie printed on it.

"Sorry—traffic on Rush St.," he cried, flinging his lab coat on over his scaly body.

But all was forgiven—that is, until he took out a shiny, gold, sparkly yo-yo and began playing with it.

"Oh, come now, Fred," protested Dr. Fitzhugh. "A yo-yo? Aren't you supposed to use a shiny gold watch hanging from a chain?"

"Never interfere with a doctor and his methods," said Dr. Samson sternly, followed by a disarming smile and a wink at the head nurse who looked away, flustered.

All eyes were upon the yo-yo as Dr. Samson let it unwind all the way and then started swinging it back and forth, back and forth.

"What is that thing?" the queen demanded. She, too, could not help but follow the yo-yo's entrancing motion.

Dr. Samson crooned, "You are getting *very* sleepy." The queen's eyelids began to droop. Even before Dr. Samson could say, "Now, when I get to the count of three," she was hypnotized.

"Does it always happen this quickly?" whispered Dr. Fitzhugh.

"I don't think so," Dr. Samson whispered back.

"What do you mean, you don't think so?" said Dr. Fitzhugh suspiciously.

"This is actually my first time hypnotizing someone."

"What?" Dr. Fitzhugh cried.

"Sh! You'll wake the queen!" said Dr. Samson.

"I wish I could wake the queen!" said Dr. Fitzhugh. "This whole thing is making me very nervous."

"But first, I've got to delve into her subconscious," said Dr. Samson. "Just stay with me; we're getting to the good part."

To the queen, he said, "Queen Esmerelda, can you hear me?"

The queen nodded slowly. Her double-lidded reptilian eyelids drooped over her half-open eyes.

"Your Majesty, we, your doctors and loyal subjects, have observed your pain. Can you tell us where it hurts?"

"In my heart," said the queen, in a quiet voice, quite unlike her usual loud one. "I'm so sad!"

"Sad? Why?" asked Dr. Samson kindly.

"I miss Meredith."

"Who's Meredith?" Dr. Samson asked Dr. Fitzhugh in a quiet voice.

"She's the queen's teenage stepdaughter," Dr. Fitzhugh whispered back hoarsely.

The queen had overheard. "Have you seen my *daughter*?" she emphasized.

"No, I haven't," said Dr. Samson, taking the lead. "Why don't you tell us about her?"

The queen's eyes snapped open. "Who are *you*?" She drew away from him. "Where's Fitzhugh? He's my doctor, not you!"

"I'm right here," said Dr. Fitzhugh, overjoyed that she had remembered him. "Go ahead, Queen Esmerelda. Tell us about Meredith."

The queen sighed, then began. "Although Meredith is my step-daughter—the late King Bertram's daughter—I love and think of her as my own daughter. It was my fault she left. We'd had an argument about politics. She didn't like the way I was running the country. When she wouldn't stop suggesting changes I should make, I told her to 'cut it out or get out.' I didn't really mean it, but she thought I did. Instead of cutting it out, she got out. That night, she stole away in secret, and I haven't seen or heard from her since."

Drs. Fitzhugh and Samson and the assembled nurses stood in respectful silence as the queen continued.

"I miss her!" she cried. "I love her ever so much! If only I could see her again and tell her how sorry I am for losing my temper! It would mean the world to me." Here she burst into torrents of salty dragon tears.

Finally, she stopped crying.

"Whew! I feel so much better, getting that out of my system," she said.

The two doctors looked at each other triumphantly.

"Now I must sleep," she announced.

"No, wait!" cried Dr. Samson and Dr. Fitzhugh together. They were too late, though. Without another word, the queen had fallen straight back onto her pile of satin pillows and fallen into a deep sleep.

That might have been all right, except that she would not wake up. Not the next day, nor the next, or even the next! The doctors tried everything. They shouted in her ears. They rang the ten loudest alarm clocks in the land. They even called in a big brass band, but she just kept on sleeping.

"George," said Dr. Samson, laying a hand on his troubled friend's shoulder, "I'm afraid it's a classic case of *Snow White's Syndrome*. See how pale she is?"

"Fred, there's no such thing as *Snow White's Syndrome*," said Dr. Fitzhugh. "Snow White was a fairy tale princess."

"Ah, but note the similarities," said Dr. Samson.

"And the differences!" cried Dr. Fitzhugh. "This isn't a fairy tale, Fred. "It's real life, and the queen's life at that. You'd better think of a solution, and fast!" Dr. Fitzhugh wrung his scaly hands together anxiously.

"Uh, now George, there's no cause for alarm—yet. Let's think positively here! If you'll just— hold— on—a—minute," Dr. Samson said, flipping through the pages of *Hypnosis for Beginners*, a book he had whipped from his lab-coat pocket. "The solution should be .... Ah, here it is, chapter thirty-five." He began to read: "When the patient has a secret desire which he or she cannot fulfill and falls into a deep sleep while under hypnosis, the only cure is—oh dear!"

"What's the matter?" demanded Dr. Fitzhugh.

"I can't make this out," said Dr. Samson. "The print is all smeared, like someone spilled water on the page. *Tsk! Tsk!*" He seemed not to notice either his wet sleeve or the overturned glass of water on the table next to him.

"Are you sure you can't read it?" asked Dr. Fitzhugh. "Here, let me see. You're right, the print is hopelessly blurred. Great! Now what are we supposed to do!"

"Calm down, George. We'll just have to find another copy of *Hypnosis for Beginners*," said Dr. Samson. "I'm sure the library will have one we can borrow. Don't worry! Why, in no time we'll discover how to awaken the queen. I'll be in touch soon. Ta ta!"

"I surely hope so," Dr. Fitzhugh said, as Dr. Samson made his swift exit.

* * *

The next day while Dr. Fitzhugh was at work at his desk, his telephone rang.

"George? Fred here. Listen, the local library doesn't have a copy of *Hypnosis for Beginners*. I've put in a request to borrow a copy from another library, though. It's to be handled through the interlibrary loan program. 'Winding Ways,' I think it's called."

"That's great!" said Dr. Fitzhugh. "When do you think it might arrive? Next week?"

"Uh—it usually takes a little longer than that," said Dr. Samson. "But don't worry, George! After the way the queen's been carrying on, she's earned a bit of a nap. I'll be in touch."

"But Fred—"

"Ta ta!" Dr. Samson said cheerily. *Click.*

CHAPTER THREE

A Mysterious Visitor

Dr. Fitzhugh set his phone down with a worried brow. He did not want to wait for Dr. Samson's book to arrive, but what else could he do?

He busied himself with his medical reports, unaware that the sun had gone down. Everyone else had gone home for the day. Everyone, that is, except a human janitor who stood in his doorway, leaning on a broom. Although he was dressed in an ordinary cotton shirt and pants, he was wearing sunglasses and a hat that came down low over his eyes.

"It's time to go home, Doctor," the man suggested kindly. He began to sweep the floor, limping as he went.

"Huh? Yes, I guess it is late." The dragon doctor took off his glasses and rubbed his tired, red-rimmed eyes.

"Say, Doctor," said the janitor. He stopped sweeping, right in front of Dr. Fitzhugh's desk.

"I'm sorry; I'm a bit busy," said Dr. Fitzhugh.

"Please, there isn't much time," said the janitor.

Dr. Fitzhugh sighed and put down his pen. "All right. What is so important?"

"This isn't any of my business, but the other palace janitors and I, well, we've been talking. We're concerned that, with the queen being sick, there's no one to rule Almira and protect us from those rebel dragons in the hills."

The doctor glared at him sternly. "These are matters which do not concern you. Now if you'll excuse me—"

"But Doctor! Don't you know who the leader of the rebel dragons is? It's *Meredith*. That's right, the queen's own daughter. If you could find her and bring her to the queen .... Don't you see what I'm saying?"

"I can't see a thing," said Dr. Fitzhugh. "Hold on a minute." The doctor yanked off his glasses and held them up to the light. "No wonder I can't see." He breathed on the lenses to clean them. Unfortunately, his hot breath melted one of the side pieces. "Why do I always do that?" he muttered under his breath, putting his mangled glasses back on as best he could.

"You sound like you've been reading the same fairy tales my friend Samson has," said Dr. Fitzhugh to the janitor. "But you're not a doctor, are you?" Dr. Fitzhugh narrowed his reptilian eyes suspiciously. "Just who are you, anyway? And how do you know so much about the rebel Red Dragons?"

"Please don't ask questions I can't answer," warned the janitor, backing towards the door.

"No, wait—please. I need your help. Tell me, whom should I send to find Meredith? Would *you* go, Mr. ...?"

The janitor hesitated, his hand on the doorknob. "Some call me 'Mr. White.' However, you probably won't see me again. I can't go, due to my bad leg. I might know someone, though, who could. Have you paper and a pencil? Thank you."

The janitor scribbled a name on the scrap of paper Dr. Fitzhugh handed him. Then he folded the paper artistically several times before handing it to Dr. Fitzhugh.

"Why, you've made a paper dragon!" said Dr. Fitzhugh.

"Open it," suggested the janitor.

"But that would spoil it!" cried Dr. Fitzhugh. Still, he was curious. Intent on his task, he started carefully undoing the paper folds, one by one. It took him awhile.

"This is a neat trick of yours, Mr. White," he said, looking up from his desk, but no one was there. He ran out into the hall, calling "Mr. White! Mr. White! Where did you go?"

"This is all very strange," said Dr. Fitzhugh out loud to himself. "His handwriting is worse than mine, but it looks like he's written: 'Send Peter Porter.' I wonder who that could be."

The doctor sighed. It had been a long, confusing day.

* * *

That night, as he was sitting at home in his comfy dragon lair, his phone rang.

"George? Fred here. Listen, I've been calling everyone I know, trying to find a copy of the book with the—er—blurred page. So far, I've talked to one hundred and fourteen hypnotists, but none of them has ever heard of it. Nor has any of them ever come across a case like this. Since it involves a queen, I think they are hesitant to get involved. If anything should happen—"

"—I know, Fred, I know," Dr. Samson interrupted. "Never mind about the book. I think we've got the answer. It's been under our fingertips all this time."

"Oh?"

"Yes. Don't ask me where I got the idea, but we've got to find the queen's daughter, Meredith, and bring her to the queen."

"I don't know, George," said Dr. Samson. "I think we ought to wait and see what *Hypnosis for Beginners* recommends."

"Let me know when your magic *book* arrives," said Dr. Fitzhugh. "In the meantime, I'm going to send someone out looking for Meredith. It's got to be done quietly, though," Dr. Fitzhugh finished, half to himself.

"Oh, and why is that?" asked his sharp-eared friend.

"Just a second." Dr. Fitzhugh pulled open the curtains and peered out the window. *What was that rustling sound in the bushes?* He yanked the curtains closed, not wanting to know whether the shadowy figure he thought he'd seen was real, or only trees moving in the wind.

"George?"

Tomorrow, thought Dr. Fitzhugh, as he absent-mindedly hung up on his friend. Tomorrow, he'd set about finding Peter Porter. The dragon doctor imagined he must be a big, strong fellow who could fight off any foe.

Little did he know ....

CHAPTER FOUR

A Job Interview

W hen Dr. Fitzhugh arrived at his office the next morning, he was surprised to find a half-grown boy standing outside his door.

"The bathroom's down the hall, sonny. Say, what are you doing here? Where's the rest of your class? Are you here on a field trip?"

"Uh—I finished school early," said Peter, dodging the question. "My name's Peter Porter." He held his hand out politely. "My mom said you wanted to see me."

"*You're* Peter Porter? How did you—why, you're just a boy!" Dr. Fitzhugh took in the boy's tousled hair, freckled, earnest face, clean-but-faded shirt, and neatly patched jeans. "How old are you, anyway? About twelve?"

"Probably too young," said Peter. "So, I'll be going—"

"—Please, won't you come in?" Dr. Fitzhugh stood in the doorway and held his office door open. Peter didn't think he had a choice. He stepped carefully over the doctor's large, scaly green feet into the dragon doctor's office.

"Sit down, Peter." Dr. Fitzhugh gestured towards a squishy, orange squash-colored chair across from his desk. Peter sank deeply into its depths, wondering how he would ever get out of it.

"Let's get right to business, shall we?" The dragon doctor rummaged in his desk drawer. "Ah, here it is." He proudly placed a folded-paper figure four inches high on his desk.

"What is that?" Peter asked politely.

"You can't tell?" The dragon doctor sounded hurt. "Why, it's a dragon, of course. You really couldn't tell?"

"I wasn't sure at first; but yes, now, I can see it," Peter said kindly.

"Then you've passed the first test," said Dr. Fitzhugh, relieved. "Peter, your name is on my 'short list' as the person to send on a sensitive mission. Folded inside this paper dragon is a secret message for Princess Meredith, the queen's own daughter. Your job—if you'll accept it—is to find her, give it to her, and escort her safely home to Almira. With any luck, you'll be home by suppertime."

"But Doctor, I don't work for the palace anymore."

"You mean you used to?" Dr. Fitzhugh asked, surprised. "This palace is so big; I can't keep track of everybody."

"Y-e-s, I used to be a palace messenger boy, but Queen Esmerelda fired me."

"You don't say," said the doctor uneasily. "Whatever for?"

"Uh—I would rather not say," said Peter.

"I insist," said the doctor.

Peter sighed. "It was for being the son of a traitor." Under his breath, he added, "but my father is not a traitor."

"Oh my!" said Dr. Fitzhugh, who had only heard the first part, "Mr. White neglected to mention this fact. Maybe we should reconsider—"

"Excuse me—did you say 'Mr. White'?" Peter broke in.

"White—Knight—something like that. A mysterious fellow. Do you know him?" asked Dr. Fitzhugh.

"Why, y—"

"—Doesn't matter. Goodness, look at the time! Peter. I think you're the one for this task. Congratulations! You're hired! Let me just seal the message." He placed his origami dragon inside a small envelope. Next, he melted some rose-colored sealing wax with his hot breath, dribbled it over the place where the flap met the envelope, and applied the official palace seal, leaving an imprint of the letter E—for *Esmerelda*—in the wax. Then he stood up and walked over to where Peter was sitting.

"You'll probably be wanting to get started right away," Dr. Fitzhugh said. He offered Peter his scaly green hand and helped him out of the chair. Then he handed him the envelope.

"Please, Doctor," said Peter, as Dr. Fitzhugh ushered him out the door. "Couldn't you send someone else? I wouldn't know where to look. After all, I'm just a—"

The doctor bent and began to whisper hoarsely into Peter's ear: "Look in the Guldavian Hills, for they say—oh, that beeper! I've got to go to a patient!"

"But—but—"

"—They say she's hiding in those hills. Here's a map." The doctor pulled a map out of his lab coat pocket and handed it to Peter. "With any luck, you'll be home in time for supper."

Map in hand, Peter watched as the doctor disappeared down the hall, his talons clicking staccato against the cold stone floor.

The Guldavian Hills! His mother would have a fit if she knew. No human ever went into those hills without good reason, for they were rumored to be full of the hidden lairs of dragon lords.

Still, "Mr. White" had recommended him. And "Mr. White," as Peter knew, was really Maxwell Porter, his own father. Thought by many to be dead, he spent his days in disguise, secretly looking out for the interests of Queen Esmerelda. He performed this thankless service loyally, even though she considered him to be a traitor because of his sympathies for the rebel Red Dragons.

We shall not meet him again—at least, not right away—for he did his work in secret.

* * *

That night, a mysterious fire broke out in the neighboring dragon kingdom of Guldavia. At the time, a princely dragon had been sitting in the Guldavia palace's counting house, totally engrossed in his favorite pastime:

"Oh, I'm in my counting house, counting out my money," the pear-shaped dragon prince sang, while picking up handfuls of gold coins and letting them slide through his thick, scaly fingers. Suddenly he noticed that the air in the counting house was getting considerably warmer. In fact, it was becoming downright stifling.

"What's wrong with that thermostat?" he thought aloud. He waddled over to take a closer look. "Daddy should have that fixed." He wiped at the beads of perspiration which dripped from his scaly brow. It was only when he went to open the window that his eye caught the gleam of flickering flames outside.

"Fire!" he screamed. "Help, Daddy! Help!"

But there was no answer. There was no one to help him. What could he do?

"The treasure!" he cried. He could at least try to protect it from being destroyed.

Forgetting everything he had ever been taught about what to do in case of fire—which was, of course, to go outside at once and not bother about trying to bring anything with you—he began gathering up all the gold he could and putting it back into the bags he had dumped it out of.

They were so heavy; he could scarcely lift them. Somehow, he managed to heave them all back into the cast-iron, fire-proof vault from which he had taken them. And just in time, too! The flames were getting closer and closer. He was terrified! How could he save himself?

Shrieking, he climbed into the counting house's fire-proof cast-iron vault, or safe. It was like a vault in a bank, the place where it keeps its treasure. He stretched out his scaly arm and pulled on the inside handle of the heavy door. Slowly, it swung shut with a clang.

Whew! He was "safe" from the fire, at least. But now what would he do?

Fortunately, he had plenty of room in which to stand up straight and move about. Also, he had enough air to breathe for the immediate future. He figured he would stay inside the vault just until the fires died down. Exhausted from his exciting ordeal, he curled up in a corner and fell asleep.

After a few hours, he woke up. All was quiet. He wondered if it might be "safe" to come out yet.

He tried the door, but it had locked when he'd pulled it shut. He had no key.

"Help! Help!" he cried to no avail. Frantically, he took off his belt and began slamming its metal buckle against one metal wall of the safe, trying to be heard.

Clang! Clang! Inside the noise was deafening. After each clang he cowered in the corner with his hands tightly over his ears. The sound reverberated from wall to wall, ceiling to floor, until the poor prince's ears tingled, and tears came to his eyes. After about an hour of this, he had developed quite a headache.

Still, he kept on clanging.

CHAPTER FIVE

A Surprising Discovery

Peter Porter tore his way through yet another bramble-strewn path in the Guldavian Hills. Cockleburs stuck to his pants legs. For several days now, he had gone out searching for Meredith, to no avail. He had not discovered even one clue as to her whereabouts. Peter suspected that people knew more than they were telling. He wondered what they were afraid of.

They should've sent a grownup on this job, thought Peter. Still, he did not want to disappoint his father (the mysterious "Mr. White") or the dragon doctor.

As usual, Peter had started out early in the day in his search for Meredith. It was now noon. The sun bore down relentlessly upon him. There was no breeze. He had gone out without a hat to protect him from the sun. He took a sip of water from his water bottle. It was almost empty. He would have to find more water soon or turn back.

Wait! Was he imagining things, or was that a well up ahead? Peter held his hand up to shield his eyes from the sun's glare to see better. Yes! It was one of those old-fashioned round stone wells with a little roof on top that are sometimes called "wishing wells." What could it hurt, Peter thought, to make a wish that he would find Meredith? But first, he would refill his water bottle. He hurried towards the well.

As he approached the well, he came upon a young woman talking earnestly to two giggling, rambunctious young children: "Kids, I mean it! Don't play so close to the well."

Peter approached them in a friendly manner. "Hello! Oh. I'm sorry; you're busy."

"Give me a minute." She settled the children down to playing "Rock, Scissors, Paper."

"You have lovely children," said Peter sincerely.

"Thank you," said the woman. "They won't sit quietly for long. How can I help you?"

"Uh—do you mind if I refill my water bottle?"

"Not at all. This is a community well. Take some from the bucket I just filled."

"Thank you." He proceeded to do so.

"I have never seen you around here before. What brings you out this way?" asked the young mother.

It was never easy to bring up the subject.

"Actually, I've been looking for Princess Meredith. I don't suppose you've seen her."

"Who?" the woman spoke sharply.

"Uh, Princess Meredith. You know, Queen Esmerelda's daughter."

"That's what I thought you said. No, I haven't seen her. If I were you, I wouldn't be asking such questions around here. They can only get you into trouble." She looked about her, as if to make sure no one was watching or listening.

"Kids, let's go. Now!" She grabbed their hands and rushed off. She left in such a hurry that she even left her water pails behind.

"Wait! Don't be afraid!" Peter called after her, in vain. *Oh well.* Frustrated, he kicked at the dirt with the toe of his scruffy boot. He cupped his hands and drank some water from the pail she had left behind. It was sweet and good. Then he splashed a little on his face and refilled his water bottle.

Thus refreshed, he headed down the path once more. What else could he do? What was it about Meredith, he wondered, that made everybody so afraid to talk to him? The path led him into a deep wood, dark and shady.

He tried singing a little tune to bolster his resolve—*dum-de-dee*. Suddenly, the song ceased on his lips, for, just ahead of him, the trees about him were no longer shady. They were stark, bare and blackened. The ground was covered with a strange gray substance. When he took a pinch of it between his fingers, it smeared into nothing. *Ash!* And not a living thing in sight. Not even one single hopping toad! What had happened here? It must have been something awful!

Stunned at the sudden desolation all around him, Peter sat down on a charred tree stump to consult his map of Guldavia. "Right here there should be a post office, on the palace grounds," he mused aloud. "But I don't see a post office or a palace. This whole place looks like it was hit by a bomb! Gee, I hope no one was hurt."

As he raised his eyes, they met those of an indignant female dragon, staring out at him from a "Wanted" poster on the remains of a crumbling brick wall. Peter thought she was quite beautiful, even though she was being depicted as ferociously breathing fire. He read the words on the poster:

REWARD!

500 gold dracos
for information leading to the capture of
Princess Meredith
for speaking out against the king's laws and
encouraging others to go against them.
By order of King Harold the Humble.

"So that's why I couldn't find her," Peter mused aloud. "She must be hiding out somewhere. I wonder what this is all about. I sure hope she didn't have anything to do with this fire." He shuddered at the thought.

He became aware of a sound in the stillness, so faint he could hardly be sure he heard it at all. *Tinkle!* There it was again. *Tinkle! Tinkle!*

What could it be? It seemed to be coming from the other side of a vine-covered, somewhat-crumbling brick wall. Peter climbed the strong vines and scaled the wall, dropping easily to the ground on the other side.

There he found, to his amazement, a huge cast-iron box, eight feet high, wide, and deep. It looked like a giant-sized bank vault. Indeed, it was a huge safe, complete with handle and combination lock. But what would a safe be doing out here, all by itself?

Tinkle! The sound was louder now. It seemed to be coming from inside the safe, of all things!

Fortunately, his father, who had trained and occasionally worked as a locksmith, had taught him how to open almost any lock. He deftly set to work "picking" this one.

As the lock sprang open, his eyes widened at the sight of a great hoard of treasure, piles of shining gold and sparkling jewels—more than he had ever seen!

But what was that pear-shaped object in the corner? In the glare of the sun, Peter could just barely make out the figure of a royal dragon (judging by his crown), cowering with his hands over his ears, a belt with a silver buckle dangling from one hand.

CHAPTER SIX

How To Handle a Prince

Ahem. Peter coughed politely.

The royal dragon youth looked at him from his crouched position, embarrassed. To Peter, he seemed enormous. He was almost twice as big as Peter and about two heads taller than his father.

"Do you mind if I ask what you are doing in this—it is a safe, isn't it?" Peter cautiously stepped inside the open door of the safe.

The royal dragon glared at Peter, putting his hands to his head. "My poor head! I've been clanging nonstop, trying to get someone to hear me. It's about time you got here. What took you so long?"

"What do you mean?" asked Peter.

The dragon youth squinted at Peter in the bright sunlight. "You *are* here to rescue me, aren't you?"

"Actually, I was just—"

"Just who *are* you, and why are you here?" the dragon demanded suspiciously.

"I'm Peter Porter."

"And?"

"I'd rather not go into the details, if you don't mind," said Peter politely.

"Tell me!" demanded the dragon, coming towards Peter menacingly.

"I've been looking for Meredith." Peter's voice faltered. "I don't suppose—"

"—Meredith! That outlaw cousin of mine! Where is she!"

"As I said, I've been *looking* for her," said Peter.

The dragon youth sprang to his full height. As he did, he banged his head on the ceiling. His pants, beltless (he had forgotten), fell to his ankles. There he stood in his purple polka-dotted undershorts. Peter stifled a chuckle.

"I'll have you know, I am *Prince* Rupert of the House of the White Dragons, son of King Harold the Humble, King of Guldavia. Show some respect!" With all the dignity he could muster, the prince bent to pick up his pants. However, as he did so, his crown fell off his head. Clang! It hit the cast iron floor of the safe.

Peter picked it up and twirled it around one finger. "Hey, it's light! What's it made of, anyway?"

"How should I know? Anyway, it's just my everyday crown."

"Here." Peter tossed it to him.

Rupert, who hadn't expected the toss, missed. The crown fell again, hard, against the floor of the safe. This time, one of its brittle points broke off. Rupert's face turned red, and angry puffs of smoke came out of his ears.

"I'm sorry," said Peter. "Good thing it was just your everyday crown."

"Hmpf! You'll go to jail for this," Rupert raged. Pushing past Peter to the door of the safe, he yelled at the top of his lungs: "Guards! Guards!" but there were no guards waiting outside to hear him and come to his aid. Undaunted, he grabbed Peter by the "scruff of the neck" (in other words, by his shirt collar).

Peter fought loose. "Cut it out, Rupert!"

"You'll pay for this," said Rupert. "Besides, you're probably a thief. Only a thief would have known how to break open this safe."

"I'm not a thief!"

"Then how do you account for your incredible safe-cracking abilities, hmm?" Rupert grabbed Peter's ear and twisted it hard.

"Ouch! Cut it out, Rupert!" Peter kicked free and took off running. However, that cunning Rupert stuck his scaly foot out and tripped him, causing him to fall flat on his face.

Rupert stood over Peter with his arms crossed, demanding: "Answer my question. How did you learn to open a safe?"

Peter picked himself up and brushed off his pants. He was beginning to wish he had left Rupert right where he had found him.

"My father taught me, if you must know," said Peter. "He learned from a correspondence course."

"Oh, really," Rupert said sarcastically. "And where is he now?"

"Now?" Peter stalled, choosing his words carefully. "I would not know, *exactly*. Since the fighting began—between the Red and the White Dragons—"

"—Which side was he on?" Rupert demanded.

"Side?" Peter stalled.

"You heard me. If he was on the side of those Red Dragons— he was, wasn't he? I knew it! Then you are the son of a traitor and shall pay for the crimes of your father as well as your own!"

"That's not fair!" Peter protested. "I never said—"

"—I'm going to put you in the dungeon and throw away the key."

"Oh yeah? Well, good luck trying to keep prisoners in *that* dungeon. Have you noticed it no longer has a palace sitting on top of it? Just look and see for yourself."

Rupert looked about him. Peter was right. All Rupert could see, no matter where he looked, were the charred and broken remains of his former grand home. Guldavia Palace was no more.

"Where did everybody go, anyway?" Rupert began waddling through the ruins looking for signs of life of any kind—human, dragon, or other. He saw no one, though.

"Daddy! Hello! Anybody?" The only answer he received, though, was the echo of his voice, returning from the hills.

"I can't handle this!" Rupert wailed, crouching down on his haunches.

Peter seized the moment. "Look, Your Highness, I don't think we should stay here. After all, what's to keep those same marauding dragons from returning and looking for survivors to capture—or worse?"

Rupert's lower lip quivered, as if he were about to cry. "What do you mean: 'or worse'?" he asked uneasily.

"Do I really have to explain?" said Peter.

"I guess not," said Rupert. "But where should I go? What should I do?"

Peter considered their options for a moment before saying, "Well, you could come home with me, I suppose. It's not too far from here, and we could leave a note for your father, King Harold, so he'll know where to find you. He'll probably be sending someone looking for you soon if he hasn't already done so."

"How far is it to your house? I can't walk far in these." He pointed to his pale green silk slippers. They were decorated with colored beads and trim in a fancy looping design. Their toes pointed into curlicues. They would never hold up on a hike across the countryside.

"Maybe you should go barefoot," suggested Peter. "It's too bad you can't fit into my boots. I'm used to going barefoot."

Rupert stared longingly at Peter's hiking boots. However, Peter was right. They were about five sizes too small for the prince, due to his long talons.

"Maybe we should trim your toenails," Peter joked.

"They're not toenails, they're talons," said Rupert, all in a huff. "And don't you dare touch them, Peter Porter! It took me years to grow them out this long."

"I was just kidding," said Peter, looking respectfully at Rupert's talons. "You know, your talons would be great for guitar playing. I don't suppose—never mind," he said quickly, as Rupert glowered at him. "Anyway, it's going to be dark soon. If you want to come home with me tonight, we should get going."

A giant owl flew overhead, hooting eerily. It swooped down ominously close to Rupert, as if it were looking for prey. Then it swept off again with a loud flutter of wings. Apparently it was having second thoughts on whether Rupert would make a good meal.

"Did you see that?" cried Rupert. "It looked like it wanted to carry me off."

"Yes. It's gone now, though." For just a moment, Peter almost wished an owl *would* carry Rupert off, so he wouldn't have to put up with Rupert's demanding ways anymore. However, he didn't *really* want any harm to come to the dragon prince. He didn't *really* want him to be carried away by a giant owl.

"Well, what are we waiting for!" Rupert shrieked. "Let's get going!"

The message to Meredith would just have to wait, Peter thought, with relief, as the two of them set out for the Porter farm. Could Meredith and her band have caused this terrible fire? That's what it looked like. And yet, his father had always spoken so highly of her.

"Dad, please be there when I get home, so we can talk about this assignment," Peter whispered, wishing his father could hear him.

"Stop whispering," Rupert snapped. "I'm listening for owls."

Chapter Seven

"It's All Your Fault!"

O
h, oh, I can't stand all these rocks!" complained Rupert for the umpteenth time. "How much farther do we have to go?" He wiped his scaly brow.

"Not too much," said Peter, climbing the hill in front of him cheerfully.

Rupert's stomach grumbled loudly. He tried to cover it up. "Did you hear that thunder?"

"What thunder?"

Rupert's stomach grumbled loudly again. He looked embarrassed.

"Oh, *that* thunder." Peter stifled a chuckle. "Yes, we'd better hurry; there must be a big storm brewing!"

Soon after that, they passed an apple tree loaded with apples. Peter picked one of its red apples and crunched into it. It tasted juicy, sweet, and good. He picked another one for Rupert.

"Here, Rupert. Are you hungry? *Catch.*"

Rupert looked up too late. The apple landed on his foot.

"Ouch! Peter Porter you'll pay for this!" Whiffs of smoke came out of Rupert's ears.

"Oops! Sorry, Rupert. Here, try again."

This time the apple hit Rupert—*thud!* —in the chest. He glowered.

"Oops! Sorry! You're supposed to catch them." Peter kept throwing apples to (or at) Rupert, and Rupert kept missing.

"Cut it out, Peter," Rupert cried, putting up his hands to protect himself.

"Sorry, I got carried away," said Peter. "But if you're hungry, why don't you eat an apple?" Peter ran ahead, then waited for Rupert to catch up.

They kept trekking along until Rupert plopped himself down and wouldn't get up.

"I can't take another step!" he cried. "My feet are killing me. Just look at these slippers. They're in shreds, and it's all your fault."

"My fault!" cried Peter.

"Yes, your fault!" replied Rupert. "You got me into this, Peter Porter. Now you'll have to carry me the rest of the way."

"Oh, come now, Rupert! That's impossible! You must weigh— well, more than I do—although it's all muscle, of course," Peter quickly added, seeing Rupert's huffy look. "No offense, but you're a dragon! Why don't you just use those wings of yours and fly?"

"Whoever told you dragons could fly?" asked Rupert. "Have you ever seen a dragon fly?"

"No," said Peter, "but in some of the books I've read, they fly. Think about it: why would dragons have wings if not to fly?"

"You ask way too many questions," said Rupert. "You're going to get yourself into trouble one of these days, doing that."

"But that's how people learn, by asking questions," Peter protested. "Never mind. Maybe now that you've rested, you could try walking again."

Grudgingly, Rupert got to his feet. They trudged on in silence, up and down the hilly land. As they got closer to the Porter farm, Peter climbed on ahead to the top of the last hill, leaving Rupert trailing behind. Peter called down to him, "Rupert, hurry! We're almost there. I can see my family's farm from here."

Rupert, however, had curled himself up into a fetal position on the grass. "Wake me up in the morning," he said with a yawn.

"Please, Rupert, do get up. It's just a little bit further!" But Rupert would not budge. Peter went back down to him and nudged him with his toe. He never expected that one nudge would send Rupert rolling pell-mell, all the rest of the way down to the bottom of the grassy hillside. With glee, Peter rolled down the hill after him.

"Wasn't that fun!" Peter said, springing to his feet.

"My crown is *totally* ruined now, thanks to you," Rupert grumbled, examining his bent-up crown.

"It does look a little like a squashed hard-boiled egg," Peter cheerfully agreed. "Here, let me see it."

When Peter tried to bend Rupert's crown back into shape, some of the jewels popped out and went flying everywhere into the tall grass.

"Now you've really done it, Peter!" Rupert shouted. Puffs of steam and smoke began to come out of his ears.

"I'm sorry," said Peter, "but you did say it was just your everyday crown."

Rupert glowered. "It was my *favorite* everyday crown," he said. "I'm not taking another step until you find those jewels, so you'd better start looking."

"But Rupert!" Peter protested. "It's getting dark out, and we're almost there. We can look for them tomorrow in the daylight. Besides, I bet they weren't even real."

More puffs of smoke and steam came out of Rupert's ears. He stamped his foot and shouted, "Real or not, you'd better get busy and find them, Peter. And I mean now!"

"Okay, okay, Rupert." Peter could not wait to get home and see his mother again. She would know how to deal with Rupert!

CHAPTER EIGHT

Peter's Mother Takes Charge

Peter was on his hands and knees in the grass as the sun was going down, looking for Rupert's missing "jewels," when he heard a familiar voice calling, "Hello! Peter, is that you?"

"Mom!" Peter was on his feet in no time.

Peter's mother came closer, her care-worn face illuminated by the soft glow of the lantern she carried.

"Peter!" she cried. "I started to get worried when you weren't home by suppertime. Oh my, I see you're not alone. Who's your friend?" she asked kindly.

"He's not my friend," Rupert muttered.

"Mother, may I present Prince Rupert of Guldavia," Peter said with a wink and a mock-formal bow.

His mother's mouth fell open in astonishment. Still, she managed a proper curtsey, as befit the occasion.

"Your Highness," she said. "We haven't much, just our farm and little thatched cottage, but you are welcome to our hospitality." They walked on towards the Porter home. No sooner had they arrived when Rupert made his first "request."

"Where's your telephone?" he demanded.

"I'm sorry, Your Highness, we don't have a telephone. Here in the country—"

34

"—No phone!" interrupted Rupert. "How am I going to call home? Never mind," he muttered. "What do you have to eat around here?"

Peter and his mother exchanged sidelong glances at Rupert's less-than-princely manners. "I've just prepared a nice hot batch of stew," she declared.

"*Yum*," said Peter.

"Yuk," said Rupert. "I hate hot food. Don't you know we Deweydaire dragons only eat cold food. My favorite is cold, cooked oatmeal."

"Cold oatmeal?" Peter couldn't believe his ears. "All sticking together and clumpy? Yuk!"

"Yum! That's the best way to eat it."

"I think we do have oatmeal," his mother broke in hastily. "If Your Highness would please excuse us .... Peter, would you please help me in the kitchen."

They left Rupert sitting on his haunches in the yard, rubbing his sore feet and lamenting his ruined slippers. In the kitchen, Peter related to his mother all that had happened.

Soon she called supper. She would serve it picnic-style in the back yard, lit by her lantern's soft light. However, Rupert was not happy, for she had put his oatmeal in an old "clawfoot" bathtub that had been "decorating" their back yard for some time.

"You don't really expect me to eat out of that, do you?" He gave the bathtub a kick with his taloned toe. This hurt him more than it hurt the bathtub.

"I'm sorry, Your Highness" said Peter's mother. "It was the only thing I had that was big enough. I thought you might be pretty hungry, after your long walk."

"Weren't you going to plant begonias in that?" Peter whispered to his mother.

"Yes, but don't worry. I washed all the dirt out of it first," she whispered back.

"Hmpf!" said Rupert. He stuck his finger into the oatmeal. "This oatmeal is still warm. How do you expect me to eat it like this? And where are the raisins and brown sugar, and the milk?"

"It will cool off soon," said Peter's mother. "I'm sorry, we don't have any raisins or brown sugar. As for milk, I'm sorry, but we don't have any just now. I haven't had time to milk the goats yet."

"Goats!"

"Yes, Your Highness, we get our milk from our goats. Here's a spoon." She handed him a rather large spoon.

Rupert watched Peter and his mother while they enjoyed their delicious, piping hot, stew. After that, they had his mom's home-made apple pie for dessert. It was too bad that Rupert didn't like stew or pie. At this point Rupert—who really was quite hungry—decided he might as well eat the oatmeal Peter's mother had prepared for him. In no time, he had polished off the whole tubful.

Then, after a loud belch— his only show of gratitude—Rupert announced, "I'm tired. I want to go to bed. Where's your guest room?" Peter and his mother exchanged glances once again at the prince's rudeness.

"Your Highness," began Peter's mother, "forgive us, for we are poor people. We don't have a room suitable for royalty, but we can offer you a room upstairs in our warm, dry stable. We have plenty of straw to make you a comfy bed. I'd be glad to make it up with sheets for you."

"Stable! Where you keep those smelly goats? Forget it!" But when he saw the steely look in Peter's mother's eye, he changed his tone to one more pleading. "Couldn't I just sleep in Peter's bed?"

"I'm not sure you'd fit," she said, being practical.

"Where is Peter, anyway?" Rupert asked.

"I don't know; he was here just a minute ago. *Peter!*" his mother called out.

"Here I am, Mother," said Peter, coming up the path with two pails full of goat's milk. "I've milked Mearsie and Dosie, just in case Rupert wants to try goat's milk with his oatmeal for breakfast."

"Mearsie and Dosie! What silly names for goats! Hee hee!" Rupert fell onto the ground, laughing hysterically.

Peter grew angry. He'd had just about all he could take of Rupert for one day. He blurted out, "There's nothing wrong with those names! Besides, it's rude to make fun of names. I don't care if they are only names for goats!"

"Hee hee—I'm sorry—hee hee," said Rupert, trying not to laugh which made it impossible for him not to. "Oh, come on, Peter. Don't you think those names are just a little bit funny?"

Peter smiled slightly. "Well, maybe they are, but my dad named those goats. I'm sure he had his reasons. I don't like anyone making fun of something my dad did."

"Speaking of your father, Peter," his mother broke in, "I need to speak to you .... if Your Highness would please excuse us for a few minutes."

Rupert grunted his permission. He was so weary, he plopped down right where he was. When Peter and his mother came out a few minutes later, they found him fast asleep, leaning against their big oak tree.

"I suppose it's just as well," said Peter.

"Yes. We're not expecting rain. It's such a pleasant evening, I wish you and I could stay outside for a while, but you've had quite a day. You're probably ready to turn in for the night." His mother took his arm as they walked toward the house. "It's so good to have you home!" she said. "Now what about this prince. How long do you think he'll be staying with us?"

"I don't know," said Peter. "I left a note, so his family would know where to find him."

When they had reached Peter's bedroom at the back of the house, he began climbing the ladder to his loft bed. "I sure was hoping Dad would be home," he said, as he lowered himself from the ladder onto his mattress. "I wanted to talk to him about this mission. I think he had something to do with it."

"Maybe so," said his mom, with a wink. "I'm sorry he's not back yet. He wanted to be here when you returned. You know how it is with his work, though. He never knows when something urgent will come up that he has to attend to."

Peter was disappointed, but he understood. It was just how things were.

"In case he couldn't get back in time, he wanted me to be sure and tell you how proud he is of you. We're both proud of you, son. Good night, now." She patted his shoulder and spread a blanket out over him.

Exhausted, Peter soon drifted off to sleep, without even changing his clothes. In his dreams, his father was there, giving him a hug that lasted just as long as he wanted it to.

CHAPTER NINE

The Prince Plays Possum

The next morning, Peter was awakened by the sound of a ram's horn, announcing the arrival of none other than Rupert's father, King Harold the Humble, and his entourage of twenty armed dragons. Peter rushed outside, just in time to see the old dragon king dismount from his chair on poles (sometimes called a *sedan chair*) which four dragons carried on their shoulders. He walked with difficulty, but dignity, toward his sleeping son Rupert who was still snoring under the tree.

"Well, don't just stand there, all of you. Somebody wake him up!" No one moved. King Harold looked about and saw his dragon servant Marcus scribbling, as usual, in his pocket-sized black notebook.

"Marcus, stop that infernal scribbling and do something!" ordered King Harold. The dragon looked up from his writing. He shrugged his wings and blew his horn, inches from Rupert's ear. Yet the prince slept on.

"Rupert!" cried the king. "Wake up. It's Dad." Rupert rolled over, opened one eye a little, then shut it again.

"Somebody fetch some cold water to splash in his face," ordered the King. No one moved. "Marcus, when I say *Somebody*, that means *you!*" roared the king. Marcus headed for the well.

"Rupert! Wake up." The king nudged his son none-so-gently with his foot. Rupert stirred a little.

"Fetch some frogs to put on him," ordered the king. "That'll rouse him."

"But sire! He hates frogs," Marcus called from the well. "Remember when Francis the Chancellor—"

"—Yes, yes," broke in the king, "I know who Francis is—"

"—made Rupert spend all day in a roomful of frogs?"

"He *did*? Whatever for?"

"To teach him to treat them kindly."

"Somebody fetch those frogs!" roared the king.

"I'm awake, Dad!" Rupert cried out. "No need for fetching frogs." But it was too late to stop Marcus from splashing a pail of ice-cold water into Rupert's astonished face. Everyone laughed—that is, everyone except for Peter and his mother—as Rupert shivered and gasped, "That's c-c-cold!"

"Yes, it is cold, and that's what you get for 'playing possum,'" said his father. "Now, down to business."

"But Dad! Aren't you glad to see me?"

"Of course I am, son! Why would you doubt it?"

"Well, you did leave me behind."

"Son, that's not fair! We looked everywhere for you. We thought you must have found a safe place to hide until the fires died down."

Rupert did not answer.

"Rupert! Were you in that counting house again? I've told you a hundred times to stay out of it. Don't tell me you hid in the safe!" King Harold looked meaningfully at his son.

Rupert looked down at his scaly feet and said nothing.

"Well, under the circumstances, it's good that you did," said the king. "It probably saved your life—but *don't do it again!* I was worried sick about you, until I found that note your friend left."

"He's not my friend," Rupert muttered under his breath. Then, addressing his father, he said, "Mom would never have left me all alone like that."

"Now, Rupert, be reasonable," said King Harold. "Your mother, may she rest in peace, never left anyone alone—*er*—anyway, I came as soon as I could. Besides, I knew—or hoped, at least—that at your age you could take care of yourself."

"This is all Meredith's fault—Meredith and those rebel dragons of hers!" Rupert cried out bitterly. "They must pay for this!"

"It does look like the work of Meredith's band," said King Harold. "We suspect those rebel dragon prisoners we took last week—the ones who were working on the chain gang in the royal fields—broke free. First, they used their balls and chains as wrecking balls to wreck most of the buildings. Then, they set everything on fire with their fiery breath."

"Leaving us without a home!" Rupert cried. "Where will we go, Dad?" Peter felt sorry for him.

"We'll stay at Rhapsody, your Uncle Ralph's castle, until our palace at Guldavia can be rebuilt," said King Harold. "You may not remember your uncle, my brother Ralph. He's been away on a genealogical expedition ever since you were a little 'tad.' Do you know what that means?"

"No," said Rupert, as if he could care less.

"Genealogy is the study of family history. Your Uncle Ralph has been away on a long journey for years, trying to piece together his 'family tree.'"

"Isn't his family history the same as ours?"

"Yes, we think so, but there are some gaps in it. Maybe he just wanted an excuse to get away from here for a while. Who knows? At any rate, we don't expect him back anytime soon."

A little crowd of country folk had gathered to see why the king and his entourage had come to the Porter farm. King Harold turned from his son to address them.

"There's a posse forming to find that Meredith, the one who told the rebels to 'fight fire with fire' after my troops ordered them to disband. I trust you'll all cooperate with law enforcement efforts."

"But, Your Majesty," said Peter to the king, his voice a brave half-squeak. "They were protesting laws they felt were unfair to the farmers. They wanted the farmers to be free to work their land in peace, to plant what they wanted and sell it to whom they chose, and to keep their profits instead of giving them all to—uh—to you, respectfully, Your Majesty. To obey your laws would have meant going against their own principles."

"Silence!" roared the king. All backed away from his fiery pronouncement. "The law is the law. I am the law. In other words, what I say goes. Now, are there any questions?"

No one dared ask any, although many stared back at him with defiant eyes.

"Be gone with you," King Harold roared. Murmuring among themselves, the crowd dispersed.

The king turned sadly to Rupert. "Son, my popularity in the kingdom is waning. I'm afraid you'll be inheriting a rabble to rule if I don't manage to bring Meredith and her band into line. If only you seemed up to the task! Why are you not interested in learning how to govern?"

"It's your fault, Dad," said Rupert, inspecting his talons in a bored fashion.

"Oh?" His dad was not so sure. "At any rate, we need to address this problem right away. How would you like a crash course in leadership? For, our monarchy may be in jeopardy. My spies tell me that some of my most trusted servants have secretly taken sides with the rebels against us, thinking they would better serve Guldavia. They want to set up what they call a 'republic' and elect their own leaders. *Representative government*, they call it."

"They could vote you out of a job, Dad," said Rupert.

"Yes, they could;" said King Harold, "and I doubt their motives. Some only want to be rich and powerful, not to serve and sacrifice if necessary. It's time, Rupert."

"Time for what?" Rupert said, yawning.

"Time for you to grow up!" said old King Harold. "In another year or so, you'll be old enough to rule in my place," said King Harold. "As you know, I am old, even for a dragon. My health ... well, I don't want you to let the country go to the rebels after I'm gone."

"Dad, since I'm the 'crown prince,' why can't I wear my good crown for everyday? This one is such a disgrace!"

"Rupert, did you hear a word I said?" The king sighed with exasperation. "Yes, you do need a new crown. I can see that. But you know we're economizing until the fighting is over between the White and the Red Dragons."

"Why?" asked Rupert. "We're rich, aren't we?"

"Not so loud! It takes a lot of money to run the kingdom, even before you start adding in the costs of fighting a war," said King Harold.

Peter, standing quietly nearby, summoned his courage to address the king.

"Your Majesty," he said, in a voice quaking with fear.

King Harold turned with mild annoyance towards Peter. "Yes? What do *you* want, young whippersnapper?"

"Before, when you were talking about Meredith ...." Peter trailed off as he saw the King wince at hearing her name. The onlookers stood by in shocked silence.

After a time, King Harold composed himself and spoke. "Princess Meredith is my niece. When she was little, I danced the *Dragon Don Derry* with her in my arms." His eyes grew misty at the memory.

Rupert tugged on his father's sleeve. "Come on, Dad. Let's go."

"Just a second, son." He continued to speak to Peter. "Grant you, Meredith is fighting for her beliefs, and I respect that. But such destruction!" King Harold shook his head in disapproval. "There must be other ways to work things out besides resorting to bloodshed and mayhem in a civilized society."

A coughing fit overcame the king. He turned aside until it had subsided.

Turning to Rupert again, King Harold said, "All right, son. Let's go."

He took Peter's mother's care-worn hand in his shaky, scaly one, kissed it, and said, "Thank you, Mrs. Porter, for your hospitality to my son." He did not see Rupert glare at her, as she curtsied, with a look that said, "You made me eat out of a bathtub."

When the king extended his gnarled hand to Peter, Rupert stepped in between them.

"Dad, this fellow is a common thief and liar. He also broke my crown! Not only that, but he's the son of a traitor. Plus, he broke into our safe. He even threw apples at me! He deserves to go to the dungeon!"

"Apples?" asked the king.

"Uh—yeah, I probably shouldn't have done that," said Peter, "but I thought he would catch them. I thought he might be hungry. I'm sorry."

"Let's leave the apples out of it, then. Even so, Rupert, you are making serious charges! It is obvious that Peter has been a friend to you. He's the one who led you to shelter when you had no place to go. Have you no gratitude?"

"Of course—but Dad! The law is the law, as you always say."

The king sighed. "Mrs. Porter, I apologize for my son's manners, or rather, his lack of them. However, he does have a point, even if one is missing from his crown. Peter, I'm afraid you must come along with us to Rhapsody Palace for questioning."

"But—but—" Peter cried out, "there are only dragons in Rhapsody. It won't be fair! It will be his (pointing to Rupert) word against mine!" Even so, Peter realized he was wasting his breath trying to argue with the king and twenty fire-breathing dragons when he stood accused by the king's own son.

"Seize him!" cried Rupert.

Tears streamed down Peter's mother's face as she bowed to the king's command.

"Have courage, son," she said. "Good things can come out of bad situations. I'll be praying for you."

"Don't worry, Mom," Peter replied bravely, like a young soldier going off to war. "I'll be back." As he kissed her goodbye, he whispered in her ear, "At least they didn't all stay for breakfast!"

"Oh, Peter." She had to smile, for even she did not have that much oatmeal on hand!

"What's so funny!" Rupert demanded.

"Nothing," said Peter and his mom together.

King Harold's servant approached them and introduced himself.

"Hi, I'm Marcus. I'll be your guard. You must be Peter." Peter looked at him warily, although he seemed friendly enough.

As the king's caravan trudged toward Rhapsody, Peter overheard several of the White Dragon foot-soldiers talking about their hopes of being chosen to join the upcoming search party. When the caravan stopped for lunch, Peter ever-so-cautiously mentioned Meredith's name to Marcus.

"Oh, so you know her," said Marcus. From his pocket, he pulled out a folded hat made out of newspaper and put it on his head. Peter could read the words *The Deweydaire Chronicle* on it. Then he took out of his pocket his small black notebook and pulled a pencil from behind his ear. "Tell me all you know," he said, with an eager look.

"Are you a reporter?" asked Peter warily.

"Let's just say, I'm always interested in a good story," said Marcus. "Tell me, how do you know Meredith?"

"I don't—I only know of her." He squatted next to Marcus who sat comfortably on his own haunches.

"Oh." Disappointed, Marcus put his notebook and pencil away and began preparing instant oatmeal for himself and Peter, using his hot breath to heat the water. After that, he let it sit a while to get cold, the way the dragons liked it.

The day was chilly for humans, but the dragons had no need of a campfire, for they were warmed by internal fire.

"I probably know more than you do—about Meredith, I mean," said Marcus as he stirred the oatmeal. "Say, are your teeth chattering? Here, sit closer to me." Peter moved closer to Marcus, grateful for the dragon's warmth which he could feel from a foot away.

"What have you heard about Meredith?" Peter asked, trying not to sound too eager.

"Well," Marcus said thoughtfully as he stirred their instant oatmeal, "I haven't seen her since her father King Bertram died. Rumor has it she's blossomed into quite an attractive young dragon maiden—if you don't mind a few *battle scars*, that is. Pity, those; I hope they don't affect her prospects for marriage. Still, her reddish-gold scales do blend fetchingly—not that I—"

"—I didn't mean *physically*," said Peter, embarrassed.

Marcus eyed Peter curiously. "What *did* you mean? Just why are you so interested in Meredith?"

Peter gulped. How much could he trust Marcus? "I'm not. I just ...."

Marcus shrugged his wings. "I hear Almira's being run by a couple of dragon doctors. Mark my words, Peter. Everything is going to be different when Meredith comes into her rightful throne. But first, she'll have to escape capture by King Harold's soldiers."

"Why, it almost sounds like you're on her side!" Peter ventured. He couldn't believe what he was hearing.

"If I am," said Marcus carefully, "I'm not the only one. After all, why should the king's word be our law? Why can't we vote and make our own laws? But it's not wise to speak of this too openly. You never know who might be listening."

Chapter Ten

"If You Leave, Don't Come Back!"

O n a nearby hilltop, a young dragon maiden crouched, peering down through the scrub brush at the caravan below. While she may have been a bit nearsighted, her hearing was as sharp as any dragon's (which was pretty darn sharp). She had, indeed, overheard quite a bit of Marcus and Peter's conversation.

"Battle scars!" she exclaimed, to no one in particular, with a contemptuous sniff. So what if she did have a scar or two? What rebel dragon didn't? Besides, she thought, you could barely see them underneath her reddish-gold scales.

Her best feature was her wings. They were transparent, as delicate as a fairy's. She had never tried to fly with them, though. As far as she knew, no Deweydaire dragon ever had. *Flying dragons? They were just in fairy tales.*

She was sure her stepmother would be appalled to learn that she was out here fighting, sacrificing her beauty and prospects for marriage. Then she stopped. Why did it matter what Queen Esmerelda thought? She would never go back to Almira Palace, never! Not after the way the queen had treated her!

After the caravan was out of sight, Meredith crept soundlessly back to her cave, where her most trusted friends and followers—dragon and human alike—awaited her.

General Abel, Commander-in-Chief of the rebel fire-breathers (commonly known as the "Fire Chief" or just "Chief") came up to her and spoke gruffly. "Well, Meredith, what did you find out?"

"Nothing we don't already know, Chief. The White Dragons are after us again."

The Chief grunted. "What do we do now, Meredith? Keep hiding, or prepare to attack again?" He rubbed his hands together eagerly at the thought of leading another attack.

Meredith's fragile wings fluttered in dismay at the thought. She took a deep breath and said, "Chief, what I'm going to say might shock you. Frankly, this fighting business has gotten out of hand. I never ordered you to attack Guldavia Palace. I never would have given such an order. Guldavia was my uncle King Harold's home. I say *was*."

"Soon we'll rid the land of all those who oppress the humans!" cried one of the rebel dragons.

"But at what cost?" asked Meredith. "I'm tired of fighting, and of running and hiding. There must be a better way of getting King Harold to listen to us than by destroying his property."

"You can't be thinking what I think you're thinking," said the Chief.

Meredith's hazel eyes, a mixture of brown, green, and gold, flashed their answer.

"Oh, Meredith!" cried Brendan, one of the rebel dragons. "You wouldn't be thinking of *surrendering*, would you?"

"Not exactly," said Meredith, "but I would like to try to work out a truce with King Harold to end this terrible war."

"But what about us?" asked Brendan.

"This isn't easy for any of us," Meredith began gently. "You've all been my faithful friends. After I leave, we may never see each other again, but I must take that chance. Tell everyone to go as far up into the hills as possible and stay there until the current interest in us blows over. It's me they're after."

"Aren't you coming with us?" asked one of the rebel dragons.

"No. I just saw King Harold and his caravan heading for Rhapsody Castle. That's where his brother, Duke Ralph, lives. I'll go there and present our demands. He must leave the human farmers with enough of their crops to feed their own families before he takes out the 'dragons' share' for taxes. In exchange, we'll agree to stop causing trouble. He'll also have to agree to call off the search party and grant us amnesty."

"Amnesty. What would that mean?" the Chief asked warily.

"It would mean a pardon for our past illegal actions. King Harold would not punish us for them."

"But Meredith, how can you trust him?" another rebel dragon asked.

"He's my uncle. He's a reasonable dragon. He'll want to stop the fighting between the White Dragons and the Red Dragons as much as I do."

"But fighting is the only life I've known," said the Chief, a little sadly.

A dragon called "Sly" slunk forward. "You were glad enough to join us, Meredith, when you came to us that night, cold, all alone, and with nowhere to go."

Meredith closed her eyes, remembering that long-ago night when she and her stepmother, Queen Esmerelda, had quarreled so bitterly. Esmerelda had shouted at her, "Either stop speaking out publicly on behalf of those human farmers or get out!" Such awful words! There was such a thing as dignity. And yet, there was a part of her that longed to make amends with her stepmother.

"You wouldn't be thinking of crawling back to her, would you?" Sly persisted.

Meredith turned away, conflicted, so they would not see her face.

"Well?" Sly insisted.

She faced the group again and said, "You should know I would never let my personal affairs come before our struggle."

"I've heard enough," cried the Chief. "What are you waiting for? If you want to go, *go!* I think you are wasting your time, though. Don't expect to come running back to us if it doesn't work out."

"You don't understand," said Meredith. "It's not like I'm betraying you, or the Human Cause."

"Who's coming with me!" the Chief threw the challenge over his shoulder as he began walking away.

Her rebel friends stared sadly at her without speaking. Then, one by one, they turned and followed the Chief; that is, all but one dragon, Brendan.

"Let me come with you, Meredith," he pleaded earnestly. "I won't cause any trouble."

"Come on, Brendan!" the Chief roared. An anguished Brendan looked first at one, then the other.

"It's all right, Brendan," said Meredith. "We'll meet again."

Reluctantly, he turned to slowly follow the rest.

"Goodbye," she called after them wistfully. "Someday, I hope you'll understand."

The Chief turned on his heel and barked out in his best battle-command voice, "You will live to regret this, Meredith."

Maybe so, but she had to go.

She stared after them until they were no longer in sight. Then she trudged slowly back to the cave she had called home since joining the rebels. She had tried to make it as homey as possible, with rugs and a few bits of furniture made from potato crates; but it was nothing like the splendor of Almira Palace where she had grown up.

The stars twinkled in the dark sky as she gathered up the few belongings most important to her. From a crate which had served as her dresser, she undid the handkerchief that held her treasured ring and put it on her finger. A gift from her beloved grandfather, it was gold, set with green peridot. She had not worn it since she had come to the rebel camp, for it was fragile. She remembered how, when it caught the light exactly right, it would cast a rainbow of colors about her, like a prism.

Next, she drew from its protective wrappings her hooded cloak of dark purple velvet. She held it up to herself, feeling its softness before putting it on, her fragile wings extending from openings in the shoulders. She twirled about in it, a princess once again.

Then she set out for Rhapsody. Alone.

CHAPTER ELEVEN

"Any Change in the Queen?"

"Has there been any change in the queen?" Dr. Samson inquired of Dr. Fitzhugh as the two dragon doctors stood at Queen Esmerelda's bedside.

"None. As you can see, she's sound asleep, as usual."

"You know," said Dr. Samson, thoughtfully stroking his scaly, dimpled chin, "I might have misdiagnosed her condition. Maybe it's not *Snow White's Syndrome* at all, but rather *Sleeping Beauty's Syndrome*."

"I don't think it really matters," said Dr. Fitzhugh drily.

"No, I suppose not," Dr. Samson agreed, upon reflection. "Although—"

"—Fred, listen. How soon before we get another copy of *Hypnosis for Beginners*? You know, the book that tells us how to awaken the queen," asked Dr. Fitzhugh, holding on to faint hope.

"Well, there have been some delays," began Dr. Samson. "The good news is, I've finally gotten my Almira library card. Now I can ask to borrow the book through the Winding Ways interlibrary loan program."

"You've just now gotten your card!" cried Dr. Fitzhugh. "What took you so long?"

"The librarian said I couldn't get a card here until I'd lived in Almira for a few months," Dr. Samson explained.

"Yes, but didn't you tell the librarian this was a *national emergency*?"

"You said not to tell anyone about the Queen because it was a secret," Dr. Samson reminded him.

"Yes, I suppose I did. Well, at least you've made the request. That's the first step."

"Frankly, George," said Dr. Samson, "I've had my doubts all along about whether that book is going to help us awaken the queen."

"Me, too, Fred," admitted Dr. Fitzhugh. "Still, why not leave the request open. In the meantime, we've simply got to keep looking for Meredith. I've had signs posted all over the countryside, but so far no one has come forward with any information."

"Apparently King Harold is looking for her too, as a wanted criminal," said Dr. Samson. "Have you seen the story about her in the *Deweydaire Chronicle*? The writer didn't put his name on it, only his initials: M-A-D. I wonder who that could be."

"M-A-D, huh. Is he mad? It might be funny if this weren't all so serious," said Dr. Fitzhugh. The two grabbed their hats and headed for the door at the same time, nearly colliding.

"After you," said Dr. Fitzhugh. "What did the story say?"

"It said most people think Meredith and her rebel dragons burned down the better part of Guldavia. Do you think she'd ever do a thing like that?"

Dr. Fitzhugh frowned uneasily, then said. "No. At least, she wouldn't unless there was no other way. You know, that young boy we sent to look for her—Peter—never came back. I wonder what became of him. Frankly, Fred, I'm extremely worried. All signs point to the fact that something's terribly wrong here, but I can't for the life of me figure out what it is."

PART TWO:
FRIENDS AND FOES

Chapter Twelve

"Which Way is Out?"

In the dreary-but-spacious Rhapsody Castle dungeon, Peter Porter paced back and forth like a caged lion. *There simply had to be a way out of this dungeon! After all, he had an important message to deliver—to Meredith!*

It did not take him long to discover everything there was to know about the dungeon. His room was one of just two, one on either side of the staircase leading to the dungeon which was the basement of Rhapsody Castle. At the top of the staircase was a door which was, of course, locked. He had plenty of room in which to move about, especially since the unlocked room on the other side of the stairs was empty—save for an occasional frog or a rat, mouse, or bug which had not yet been caught in a trap. Heavy, swinging doors opened at the base of the stairs into each of the two rooms.

The empty room was just like Peter's in many ways. It had a small, high, rectangular window which let in some—but not a lot—of light. Along the south wall, it had a broad stone ledge which contained a straw-filled mattress for sitting and/or sleeping. Poking around a bit more, he discovered—just "off" the empty room—a small storage room, a pantry, where bins of grain and piles of potatoes were being kept. Aside from a few empty potato crates stacked in a corner, that was all there was to the dungeon.

As Peter realized, his prospects for escape did not look good—not at all! He could not reach the window in his room, even if he stood on an empty potato crate. At least there *was* a window. After he wiped the dust from the glass, he could tell what time of day it was by the position of the sun. He was getting good at reading the shadows created as the light hit a stone post in the courtyard, making his own personal sundial.

Right now, it was sundown. His guard still had not come with his supper. He wondered if it would be cold-and-clumpy oatmeal like last night or cold-and-lumpy mashed potatoes like the night before. Like most humans, he preferred to eat those foods hot. Unfortunately for Peter, the dragons served everything cold.

At least some of the time, though, Peter suspected there was someone in the kitchen who was "looking out for him." Sometimes he would find apples, oranges, or bananas or crunchy raw vegetables on his tray. On those days, too, his oatmeal or mashed potatoes would likely be served piping hot. Although Peter never knew who his benefactor was, he was grateful. But oh! What he would have given for a taste of his mom's home-cooking!

When it grew dark, and still no one had come with supper for him of any kind, Peter began to worry that they had forgotten all about him. He curled up under his blanket and tried to forget his hunger pangs. He had expected better treatment than this from King Harold! Eventually, he fell asleep.

The next day, he awakened to an unfamiliar voice on the stairs.

"Oh, Peter! Yoo-hoo!"

It was Rupert!

"Down here. Where else would I be?" Peter called out, but faintly, weak as he was from hunger.

Rupert brushed through cobwebs as he entered, trailed by Marcus who had his pen and notebook ready—just in case he was called upon to take notes.

"So, what do you think of the dungeon?" Rupert asked Peter.

"I could take it or leave it, preferably leave it. But I shouldn't be here too long, right, Rupert? Just until my trial. By the way, when will that be?"

"Trial? Oh, that. Hmm, I forgot to speak to Francis the Chancellor about that. He's in charge of scheduling. He was away on a vacation, but he's back now. I confess, talking to him about you completely slipped my mind!" Rupert touched his taloned finger to his cheek in mock dismay. Then he took a chocolate candy bar from his pocket and began to slowly unwrap it, as Peter looked on hungrily.

"Oh—did you want some?" Rupert asked.

"If you don't mind," said Peter politely.

Rupert broke off a tiny triangle from the corner and handed it to him.

"Thank you." Peter let it melt on his tongue. The sugar rushed to his hungry brain, aiding his thinking process.

"Rupert, I've been in prison for two days now, and I'm still not sure why I'm here. Your father King Harold said I had to come along for questioning, but no one has asked me any questions yet. Am I being charged with any crimes?"

"Sure," said Rupert. "Don't you remember? Breaking my crown, being the son of a traitor—that sort of thing." He spun on his heels towards Marcus and said, "Marcus, are you taking notes? Add kidnapping to the list of charges."

"Kidnapped!" cried Peter. "I never kidnapped you! I rescued you! You're making things up!"

Rupert's face turned red and angry puffs of smoke came out of his ears. "Marcus, add conspiracy to the list," he ordered.

"Conspiracy! What is that?"

"If you'll permit me, Your Highness," Marcus piped up. He flipped to a page in his notebook and read: "Conspirators are guilty of the crimes of their fellow conspirators.'"

"Okay ... but what's a conspirator?" asked Peter.

"Let me see that notebook." Rupert grabbed for it.

"I just copied it from the dictionary," said Marcus, holding the notebook behind his back and away from Rupert.

"I don't care what the dictionary says," huffed Rupert. "Peter is one of Meredith's band of cut-throats, so he's just as guilty as the rest of 'em."

"But I've never even met Meredith! Or any of her band!" protested Peter.

Dodging Rupert, Marcus read from his notes: "'A conspiracy is when two or more individuals agree to commit an illegal act and take at least one step, known as an overt act, towards the goal of commission of that illegal act.'"

"Marcus, give me that notebook!" Rupert grabbed for it, but Marcus nimbly leaped aside, evading his grasp.

Peter was dumbfounded. "But I've never made any agreements with Meredith. I've never tried to help her or her band of rebels. I was sent to look for her, but I couldn't find her. So, how do you figure I was in conspiracy with her?"

"Ask the judge, if you ever get a chance," Rupert said with a smirk.

Just then a small toad, resident of the dungeon, hopped out of Peter's pocket and onto Rupert's head.

"*Ew!* Get that thing off me!" Rupert cried, brushing the hapless toad away. "Let's go, Marcus. Right now! And stop taking notes on everything."

With a sympathetic shrug of his wings as he caught Peter's worried look, Marcus followed Rupert up the dungeon stairs.

* * *

After several days, Rupert reappeared without warning.

"Peter," he said, "If I let you come upstairs, will you play with me? Felix won't."

"Who's Felix? Another boy like me?" Peter hoped for a friend.

"No, he's the court jester—a dragon of course. He says he'd rather play *Solitaire* than play with me because I cheat."

"Do you?"

Rupert forced a weak laugh. "You should know me better than that! Heh heh. So, will you come? Please!"

"Oh, I don't know." Peter pretended indifference, but his heart was beating wildly at the thought of the escape possibilities if only he could manage to get upstairs. "What all do you have to do?"

"Oh, everything. We have a regulation-size swimming pool, ping pong, racquetball—just about any game you could think of!"

"Marbles?"

"All lost," said Rupert sadly. "What's so funny?"

"Nothing. Never mind, I'll come." Peter got up to follow Rupert, but suddenly, he felt faint. Weak from hunger as he was, he stumbled and fell.

From the top of the stairs Rupert yelled down at him, "What's the matter? What are you doing down there on the floor?"

"I'm hungry!" cried Peter weakly. "I need food! Something besides cold oatmeal porridge, please! I feel like Goldilocks in *The Three Bears*."

"What's wrong with oatmeal? I love it cold," said Rupert.

"Nothing's *wrong* with it," said Peter. "I like it fine. But not every single day and not when it's served cold. Oatmeal can be good, but so can other foods. I'd love a hamburger."

"Is that vegetarian? You know we dragons are vegetarians."

"Yes, but I'm not a dragon," said Peter. "Okay, how about a fried egg sandwich, then?"

Rupert, who had never heard of a fried egg sandwich, puzzled over that a little, his forehead puckering with the effort, until the light began to dawn. "You can have anything you like! I'm sure Marcus can find the recipe. Now come on, slowpoke." He came down the stairs and grabbed Peter by the hand, pulling him up the stairs. "If you want a hamburger, that is."

"And a bath," added Peter.

"Don't press your luck. Oh, all right, but you look clean enough to me. But after that, you'd better watch out, 'cause I'm going to beat your socks off at ping-pong!" Rupert swung a pretend racket wildly, narrowly missing Peter's head.

We'll see about that, thought Peter.

CHAPTER THIRTEEN

A Rude Welcome

While the "jack-of-all-trades" servant Marcus was eagerly pouring over the pages of an old cookbook he'd discovered in the castle's attic called *Fantastic Recipes*, Peter was heading upstairs to have his bath. At least, that was what he wanted Rupert to think. In fact, while the bath water was running, he had been busy prying open the bathroom window. He was now poised on the window ledge, trying to figure out how many Rhapsody Castle towels he would need to tie together to make a "rope" long enough to reach the ground below.

"Halt!" Peter looked down just in time to see two dragon guards running back to their posts. Standing at their gates waited a tired, but determined-looking, dragon maiden. In her taloned hands, she held up two pieces of a "Wanted: Meredith!" poster she had just torn down. Despite her dusty, travel-worn appearance, she held her head high.

"Who goes there?" Peter heard one of the guards say.

"Don't you recognize me?" She held the two pieces of the poster up together.

"Meredith!" they said scornfully. "Don't you know there's a penalty for tearing down the king's *Wanted* posters? We have orders from Prince Rupert to arrest you on sight!" the head guard said, roughly clapping handcuffs onto her wrists.

"Rupert! Why? Where's King Harold?" Meredith asked.

"He died last night, in his sleep, of old age. The king is dead. Long live the king!"

Peter nearly fell out of the window in shock. *King Harold was dead! And Rupert was on the throne! What could be worse?*

"I am sorry to hear such sad news," said Meredith, "but you should know that Rupert cannot succeed his father on the throne. Why, Duke Ralph—"

"—Save your breath," said the guard. "If you had kept in touch with your family, you would know that the duke is still away on his genealogical expedition. For better or worse, Prince Rupert is in charge. Now come along! We're taking you straight to his throne room."

Peter dashed madly from the bathroom to the top of the stairs, where he crouched behind a balcony railing and peered down into the throne room below. There, Rupert sat, intently playing chess with a dragon court jester dressed in a garment of colorful patches, all gaily sewn together in "jester's motley," wearing a cap of bells on his head. Just then, Peter heard a commotion in the hallway outside the throne room.

"Take your hands off me!" Meredith twisted away from the guards as they led her before Rupert.

"Sire." The head guard bowed low.

Rupert looked up impatiently. "Yes, what is it? Oh, come in, come in. Say, this is better than I'd expected! This is only my first day on the throne, and Meredith's already been taken captive!"

"Hello, cousin." Meredith's voice was strained. "I'm so sorry to hear about your father's death. This must be such a sad time for you—"

"—Guards," Rupert butted in, "how did you capture her? Was she trying to sneak in?"

"Yes—uh, actually, no, Your Highness," the first guard said, after catching Meredith's fiercely indignant expression. "She even told us her name."

"Hmpf! Well, cousin," said Rupert, "I must say, I thought you were smarter than this! What were you thinking of, surrendering?"

"I came to seek a truce with your father," Meredith began. "I had tremendous respect for him. He was a fair and worthy opponent, although he was stubborn at times."

"*Stubborn!* How dare you insult the memory of my father!"

"Forgive me, Rupert, I mean no harm, only to speak the truth as I see it."

"*Seize her!* Into the dungeon with her!"

"But Rupert!" Meredith protested, as the guards led her away. "Won't you even listen to me?"

"On with the game, Felix," Rupert roared. But Felix could not take his eyes from Meredith.

"Felix!" cried Rupert. "What's wrong with you? Come on, it's your move! Oh, never mind. I'll just get Peter to play with me."

Rupert called upstairs, "*Yoo hoo*, Peter! Have you finished that bath yet?"

CHAPTER FOURTEEN

"What Kind of Joke is This?"

"ath." The word jolted Peter, still crouched at the top of the stairs, back to his senses. He hastened back down the carpeted hallway to the bathroom. He had flung open the door and was about to shed his bathrobe when—*oh no!* He had left the water running! It was overflowing the sides of the tub and running all over the bathroom floor. Rupert would not be pleased! He turned off the faucet, grabbed up all the towels he could find (he had to untie the ones he had joined into his towel "rope"), and started mopping up the floor.

Meanwhile, downstairs, Rupert and Felix had resumed their chess game. However, as luck would have it, Rupert's chair was directly underneath the upstairs bathroom. Before long, water had begun to soak right through the ceiling and onto his head. First, one drop plinked noisily off his crown, then another, and another, until Rupert could ignore it no longer.

As usual whenever anything went wrong, Rupert tried to blame someone else.

"What kind of joke is this, Felix!" cried Rupert.

"Joke?" Felix asked innocently.

"Don't try to play dumb with me, Felix!"

"All right, Rupert, the game is over." The jester pushed his chair back from the table with a screech. "I told you I wouldn't play with you if you cheated or started an argument with me over nothing."

"What do you mean, *nothing*?" Rupert demanded. "Don't you feel drops of water on your head?"

Just then, a large drop of water plunked down noisily onto Rupert's metal crown. Felix tried not to smile.

"I don't feel a thing, Sire," said Felix, "but I do think you have a leak upstairs."

As Rupert looked up, another drop splashed down on his nose. "Where's all the help around here?" he roared. "Somebody fix that leak!"

Peter had already turned off the faucet. Hearing the "help" come thumping up the stairs, he quickly pulled off his clothes, jumped into the bathtub, and began to wash himself—just as six of the prince's dragon servants—led by Marcus—burst into the room. Three of them held mops and buckets, while the other three wielded pipes and wrenches.

"Does a closed door mean nothing to you dragons?" asked Peter, submerging all but his head under the sudsy water.

"Where's that leak!" Marcus demanded. "Oh, it's you, Peter! What are you doing up here—oh, never mind. Sorry." He hastily ushered the confused servants out one door, just as Rupert barged in the other.

"Peter Porter! What are you trying to do, drown me?" Rupert demanded.

"Hey, Rupert, I'm sorry about the water. It was an accident—"

"—No apologies accepted. I thought we could be friends, but I can see that you're just not cut out to be a royal dragon's friend. Anyway, I've got Felix to entertain me now, so I don't need you."

"I thought you said he wouldn't play with you," said Peter. "What about our ping-pong game?"

"Cancelled," said Rupert, "so get back to the dungeon. Now! Er … just put your dirty clothes back on for now."

The dungeon! That's where they had taken Meredith. Peter dressed in a hurry. Ironically, Peter now wanted nothing more than to return to the dungeon. At last, he would get to meet Meredith! But he did not want Rupert to know how eager he was, so he tried "reverse psychology" on him.

"Oh, Rupert, please don't send me back to the dungeon," Peter begged. "You know how much I hate it, with all those cobwebs and spiders."

Rupert fell for it. "Get going this very minute," he ordered. "Guards! Escort Peter back to the dungeon."

"You don't have to do that," said Peter. "I know the way." He dragged his feet and hung his head for show. But, as soon as he was out of Rupert's sight, he began to run eagerly. He did not stop until he reached the dungeon doors.

They were heavy, iron doors. Peter pulled and pulled, but he couldn't get them to budge. *Of course! They were probably locked.* Frustrated, he slumped down, his back against the door, to wait for Marcus, his designated guard. No doubt he would be along soon with a key.

Suddenly, as if by magic, the doors opened automatically. Peter, who had been leaning against them at the time, was quite surprised. He nearly fell onto the stairs on the other side. Fortunately, he caught himself in time. He scooted onto the other side, just before the doors automatically closed again.

I wonder how that happened, thought Peter. *Did I lean up against a secret button or use a secret password without meaning to?* There was no time to spare for figuring that out, though, when he was on his way to meet Meredith.

The stairway was dark, lit only by flickering candles held in sconces along the walls. He was careful not to fall, even in his haste, as he made his way down the stairs.

Meanwhile, Felix, the court-jester, had been speeding down

the hallway on his unicycle, just as the dungeon doors had opened automatically for Peter. He blinked in amazement.

How did he do that? Felix wondered. But what good was it to let yourself back into the dungeon? Getting out was what was important. Still, the information might prove useful. Felix said nothing as he pedaled down the hallway.

Suddenly Rupert came around the corner. He was heading right into Felix's path. Screech! Felix stopped too fast to avoid hitting him. Felix lost his balance and fell off his unicycle onto the hard stone floor. Ouch!

"Felix, did you see Peter?" Rupert demanded, without even asking whether Felix was okay.

"Yes, Your Highness," said Felix, rubbing his elbow. "If that is all, I'll be on my way." He hopped onto his unicycle and began to pedal at top speed.

"Felix! Stop that thing at once!" The jester screeched to a halt again, his hat-bells jingling.

"Did Peter get back into the dungeon?" Rupert demanded.

"Yes, Your Highness," the jester said with a bow, making excuses as he raced away before Rupert could ask him any more questions.

Later, in the servants' quarters, Felix related the day's events to Marcus.

"Of course, I didn't tell Rupert what I saw," confessed Felix.

"Did he ask?" questioned Marcus.

"No," said Felix. "Now, Marcus, don't give me that look. After all, what harm can there be in Peter's being able to get into the dungeon, so long as he can't get out? By the way, what's that you're writing?"

"Oh, nothing." Marcus suddenly stopped scribbling. He shoved his black notebook into his pocket and his pencil behind his ear.

"Now, Marcus, don't you dare breathe a word of this to anyone," Felix warned.

Marcus looked up at him innocently. "What do you think I am, a blabbermouth?"

CHAPTER FIFTEEN

The Son of an Old Friend

The door at the bottom of the dungeon stairs swung open easily at Peter's touch. There, for the first time, he saw her. She was standing with her back to him, looking up at the meager little window, her hands folded serenely as if in prayer. Peter blinked hard. *Whew!* For a moment there, she had looked almost human. He stayed very still. Finally, she sensed his presence and turned around, startled, catching herself before she might have cried out.

"I'm sorry if I scared you." Peter extended his sun-browned hand toward her. "Peter Porter's the name."

"I'm Meredith."

"Just Meredith?"

"Well, our family name is Burney, but we don't use it," Meredith said.

"No, no, I mean—"

"Titles? You don't have to address me as 'Your Highness,'" she said with a gentle smile. "Just Meredith will be fine. In fact, I prefer it."

Peter found her to be quite beautiful, especially when she smiled. Unlike many of the humans in Peter's poor village, she had nice teeth (for a dragon). Yes, she had a few battle scars, but they were not so noticeable. It was not so much her physical appearance as an inner beauty that radiated from her that attracted Peter. He was not even sure she was aware of the effect she was having on him.

"Please, have a seat," said Meredith.

"Thank you," he said, taking a seat on a sturdy upturned potato crate.

She was staring at him. "There's something about you. You remind me of someone, but I can't think who it is."

"Could it be my father, Maxwell Porter?" Peter asked her.

"Yes!" said Meredith. "I should have known! You look just like him—sorry, you're probably used to hearing that."

"Well—"

"—That's a compliment, by the way," added Meredith.

Peter blushed. "Thank you."

"You're welcome. Your father was a smart, brave man," Meredith continued. "He was an army medic when I knew him and a good friend to the Red Dragons. I served at his side as a nurse for a time. Together we cared for the wounded, under the banner of the Red Cross. You must miss him terribly."

Peter leaned forward earnestly. "I do, Meredith, but he's not dead, Meredith, as everyone thinks. He's recovering from his war injuries. He still has a slight limp. That doesn't stop him, though, from looking out for Queen Esmerelda's interests, even though she considers him to be a traitor. That's why he's in hiding. He was last seen posing as a janitor at Almira Palace."

"A *janitor!*" Meredith stared incredulously at Peter; then they both burst into peals of laughter at Peter's father's daring and cleverness. "How fitting, for your father is wise and prudent like Janus, the doorkeeper god in old stories who looked both forward and backward. Tell me, Peter, what brings you to this 'fair haven'? You haven't joined forces with the rebels, have you?"

"Oh, I almost forgot!" Peter fished his hands into his pants pockets, but they came up empty.

"That's funny. I thought I had it right here. I wonder what could have happened to it?"

"To what?" Meredith asked.

Peter looked embarrassed. "I—uh—had an important message for you from Dr. Fitzhugh."

"Dr. Fitzhugh, the Almira Chief Palace Physician! Do you know what it was about?" She bit her lower lip, fearing the worst.

"I'm sorry; I don't," said Peter. "The doctor sealed it before I could find out. I'm afraid I must have lost it." Peter felt terrible.

"What do you think happened to it, Peter?"

"I don't know. I thought I had it in my pocket, but maybe I put it in my backpack. Yes, now I'm sure that's what I did. The guards took my backpack from me when they brought me down here to the dungeon—which means your letter's now in Rupert's hands!"

"Just my luck," said Meredith in dismay.

"I'm sorry, Meredith," said Peter.

She gave him a faint smile. "Oh, Peter, I know it's not your fault. I do wonder, though, what Dr. Fitzhugh wanted to tell me. I hope nothing is wrong at home."

"Maybe we can get the message back, if we let King Harold know—oh, I forgot." Peter felt awkward.

"So, you've heard," said Meredith. "Yes, King Harold the Humble is dead. Oh, I know, in some fairy tales, dragons never die. Unfortunately, they do in Deweydaire. Although, it was strange. Yesterday, I thought I saw King Harold's image in the clouds. It was probably just my imagination, but it was a comfort to me, just the same."

Peter nodded. "Poor King Harold! Maybe he wasn't always right, but he did at least try to be fair. Unlike—"

"—someone else we both know," Meredith finished. "Now, Peter, tell me *your* story. Maybe hearing it will take my mind off my troubles."

Peter sighed. "I am here awaiting trial, for Rupert has accused me of various 'crimes' such as lock-picking and breaking a point off his crown."

"How easy it is to run afoul of Rupert!" said Meredith. "What's your side of the story?"

"Rupert got himself locked in a safe, and I got him out," said Peter.

Meredith stared at him in disbelief. "I see. And so, in his 'gratitude,' he brought you here." The irony was not lost on either of them.

"Yes, but now I have found you." Peter looked at her admiringly.

"For all the good it's doing us." Meredith made a wry smile. Then, seeing Peter's hurt look, she hastened to add, "If I have to be locked up in a dungeon with someone, there's no one I'd rather be with than you."

"Aw, thanks," said Peter. "I was surprised to see the guards taking you into custody, Meredith. "From the stories I've heard, you'd never been captured."

"I wasn't captured," she said. "I came here freely to offer terms of peace to my uncle, King Harold."

Peter's eyes opened wide. "You mean you gave yourself up?"

"Not exactly," said Meredith. "I came here seeking peace, hoping a truce with Harold would stop the fighting between the White Dragons and the Red Dragons."

"That will never happen, now that Rupert is on the throne," Peter predicted, "for he is ruled by his greed, and by his advisors. Tell me, does Rupert have any rightful claim to the throne?"

"It's complicated. In Harold's 'Will'—which I once saw—he named Duke Ralph as regent. That means Ralph is supposed to rule Guldavia until Rupert proves himself mature and capable of governing. Knowing Rupert, that might take a while. However, I just found out that Duke Ralph is away on a genealogical expedition. With Ralph away, there's no one here to challenge Rupert's claim. It looks like we're stuck with Rupert until Duke Ralph gets back."

"Oh no! Isn't there anything that can be done?" asked Peter.

"No, not unless someone brings a petition asking Francis the Chancellor, the highest judge in the land, to appoint someone else to serve as regent until Ralph's return. I might have brought such a petition, but I can't do it now."

"Sh!" Peter whispered. "Someone's out there." He rose to his feet soundlessly and pushed open the swinging door to Meredith's cell. The door banged into a rather embarrassed dragon, dressed in jester's motley and wearing a cap of bells. He had been crouching outside the door, listening.

"Eavesdropper!" Peter said with scorn.

"No—yes, but I'm a friend," the dragon jester pleaded as he sprang to his feet.

"How do we know—" began Meredith. Then she looked into his eyes.

"It can't be," she cried in amazement. "Felix, former court jester from Almira! What are you doing here?"

"Here to offer my services, dear lady," Felix addressed her with a bow.

"Thank you, Felix. They may very well be needed. But your timing is off. The guard said he'd be bringing my supper soon. You'd better go. We don't to want to arouse unnecessary suspicions."

"Er—it's not that simple," said Felix, suddenly realizing that the secret button he had used to get *into* the dungeon was now on the *other* side of the door.

"Why not?" asked Meredith. "Oh, it's too late, I hear him coming."

Felix panicked. "Where can I hide?"

"Quick! Hide behind that pile of potatoes. Oh, there's no time!" said Meredith.

"Felix, what are you doing down here!" exclaimed the burly dragon guard as he burst through the swinging door into Meredith's dungeon chamber.

Felix smiled disarmingly. "Just making sure the prisoners are secure. No need to thank me. I was just leaving." Following the guard up the stairs, he turned towards Peter and Meredith, wiping his forehead in a quick, broad gesture of relief.

* * *

A few days passed without any further sign of Felix.

When he finally reappeared, he was on official duty, delivering a message for the Palace. "Peter, Rupert wants to see you."

"Is it time for my trial?"

"Maybe. I don't know."

It was not. Instead, while seated on his throne, Rupert told Peter that the only way he would even *have* a trial would be if he started spying on Meredith and telling Rupert everything he learned about her plans.

"But she doesn't *have* any plans," Peter protested.

"I refuse to believe *that*," said Rupert with a sneer.

"Rupert, you have to give me a fair trial. It's the law of the land!"

"Not anymore," said Rupert, shaking his head for emphasis. "*I'm* the law of the land now!"

Just then Francis the Chancellor, the highest (and only) judge in the land, entered the throne room. He had overheard enough of the conversation to understand exactly what was going on.

Up until now, he had not even known there was a young lad in the dungeon awaiting trial, or of the charges against him.

Now, regardless of what Rupert thought, he was not the law of the land. The real law of Deweydaire still gave everyone, be they human or dragon, the right to a fair trial. Rupert had not yet managed to wipe that law from the books.

"Prepare my courtroom for trial immediately," the chancellor ordered. Everyone concerned made haste. Peter would not have a lawyer, for that was not how things were done in Deweydaire. Rather, he would tell his story before the chancellor and a jury of four dragons who would decide his guilt or innocence.

Peter had asked to be tried by a jury of humans, but that was not how things were done in Deweydaire. Peter felt he had little chance of justice, especially since Rupert would soon be crowned king.

There was a popular saying at the time that "The king can do no wrong." It was not true, of course. Nevertheless, it was widely believed by dragons and humans alike.

Dragons and humans—alike? Yes, in many ways. For, despite their obvious differences, each species is equally intelligent. Dragons cry just like humans when they stub their toes or get their feelings hurt. They laugh when they are happy and "fume"— more or less—when they are mad.

Of course, there are some who say there are no such thing as dragons, simply because they have never seen them.

They certainly seemed real enough to Peter, though, as he stood before a jury of four of them, trying to convince them of his innocence. Once he tried closing his eyes to see if he could make them go away. But when he opened his eyes, they were still there, glaring at him in a most uncivilized way.

CHAPTER SIXTEEN

"Tell us the Truth"

Where did you learn to pick locks, young man?" the head dragon juror, or "foredragon," as he was called (the dragon version of the jury foreman), demanded. He was the one the other jurors had chosen to speak "for" them. At that time in Deweydaire, jurors were allowed to question witnesses.

Now, Peter had already answered that particular question. These dragon jurors kept asking him the same question—over and over again—as if they were trying to catch him in the act of changing his story. Francis the Chancellor kept telling them sternly to only ask any given question one time.

Peter *wanted* to tell the truth. Yet, whenever he mentioned his father, the dragon jurors would murmur amongst themselves and exchange knowing glances, as if they had already determined his guilt—even though the chancellor had told them to wait until they had heard all the evidence before they made up their minds.

Peter could not make them understand that, even if his father *were* a traitor—which he was not—that did not mean that he, Peter Porter, was a traitor. He had no lawyer to speak for him in court, for such was not yet the custom in Deweydaire.

"Please answer the question," said the chancellor, peering down at Peter over the top of his glasses from his high seat at the front of the room. He wore a long black robe and a white barrister's wig (much like barristers wear today). All ears—dragon and human alike—were cocked to hear Peter's answer.

Peter gulped. In a voice quavering with fear, he began: "You see, my family was poor, because the White Dragons wouldn't—I mean, we weren't allowed to plant any crops until we'd paid our 'back taxes'—that is, money we owed to Rhapsody Palace from past years. To help earn some money, so our family wouldn't lose our land, I became apprenticed to ... a locksmith."

Three of the jurors even nodded their approval of Peter's industrious ways. But then, from the doorway, a belligerent royal voice was heard. "I thought you told me your father taught you how to pick locks."

It was Rupert!

"Silence!" ordered the chancellor, banging his gavel. "Oh, Your Highness, I didn't know it was you! Well, silence anyway!" To Peter he sternly said, "Young man, is this true?"

"I'm afraid so, your Honor," Peter reluctantly admitted. "But what I said before was also true."

"Oh? Please explain," said the chancellor.

"I'll try. You see, my father had passed the training and occasionally worked as a locksmith. It was just one of his occupations—"

"—*Spy* being another one!" interrupted Rupert.

The chancellor banged his gavel and addressed Rupert: "Your Highness, I must implore you not to speak out."

"Your Honor, I have a question for Peter, if I may," said the foredragon.

"Certainly, proceed."

The foredragon cleared his throat and began: "Young man, have you ever before used your lock-picking to break the law?"

Now, this was the question Peter had been dreading. *Oh, why couldn't the past remain buried where it belonged?*

"Sure, he has," Rupert answered for him.

The chancellor's expression grew stern. "Your Highness, I've told you twice to keep still. Now I must ask Marcus to serve as bailiff and remove you from the court. You are disturbing the proceedings."

"Wha—what?" Rupert could not believe his dragon ears. In a daze, he allowed Marcus to lead him from the courtroom.

"Now, my boy," the chancellor said, "You may answer: Have you ever used your knowledge of lock-picking to break the law?"

"Once," Peter admitted reluctantly. "You see ...."

"Go ahead," the chancellor encouraged him in a kindly voice. "Tell us."

Peter gulped. "Well," he began, "once I did find a dragon's treasure chest. I couldn't resist prying it open." The jurors began murmuring again amongst themselves and glaring at him.

"Silence!" The chancellor banged his gavel again. "Peter, did you take any of the treasure from the chest?"

"Uh—just a little. You see," Peter hurried to add, "we needed money to buy medicine for our goats. That year our crops had failed. Mom was exhausted, and Dad was away, serving in the war between the White and the Red Dragons as a medic. There was so much treasure in the chest, I didn't think the little bit I took would be missed."

Shocked silence filled the room. "I was caught," admitted Peter, "tried, and punished. I'm sorry and ashamed of what I did. I've learned my lesson; I've never been in trouble since then. That is, until now."

The jurors stared at him with distrust. They began to murmur among themselves.

Peter's voice was shaking, but he spoke out bravely: "Just because I did something bad once before doesn't prove I'm guilty this time, does it?"

The jurors looked at one another uneasily.

"No, Peter it does not," said the chancellor. "Does anyone have more evidence to present? If not, would the jurors please go to the jury room and make your decision. Do you find Peter guilty or innocent of the crimes with which he has been charged? The jury room is down the hall and to your left."

"*Ahem*," the foredragon cleared his throat. "That won't be necessary, Your Honor. We've already made up our minds."

"You can't make up your minds until you've first discussed the evidence among yourselves," said the chancellor patiently. "Go to the jury room and talk among yourselves. Discuss the strengths and weaknesses of the evidence. Listen to one another before you decide. That way, Mr. Foredragon, when you deliver the verdict, you will be speaking for the entire jury, not just for yourself."

"Yes, Your Honor," said the foredragon, shrugging his winged shoulders.

The dragon jurors followed the foredragon to the jury room. In only half an hour, they were back.

The foredragon addressed the chancellor: "Your Honor, we have our verdict."

"That was not very much time. Are you sure?

"Yes, Your Honor."

"Very well, then. Please state it for the record," said the chancellor.

"'We find the defendant *guilty*," the foredragon announced. All the dragons in the courtroom roared their approval.

"Order in the court!" demanded the chancellor, banging his gavel. "Peter Porter, would you please stand up."

Peter stood, trembling, wondering why he had expected anything different from a dragon jury.

"Peter," began the chancellor, "the jury has found you guilty.

Therefore, guilty you are, under the strict laws of Deweydaire. However, as chancellor, I also have inherent powers to 'do equity.' In Deweydaire, the law must be both fair and just. Consequently, I am overturning the jury's verdict because I find that it is not supported by the evidence. Moreover, I find that the jury was biased against you. I therefore declare you *not guilty*. You are free to go, my boy."

The dragon jurors stared at the judge in disbelief, their mouths gaping open.

"But Your Honor—if I may ask—why?" the foredragon asked.

"Because these are the most ridiculous charges I have ever heard! Peter only broke into the safe to free Rupert. He's no thief!"

"But Your Honor—if I may—only a thief would possess such lock-picking skills," protested the foredragon.

"He was the son of a locksmith," the chancellor patiently reminded him.

"You mean, the son of a traitor," the foredragon muttered.

"Peter is not being tried for his father's crimes, only for his own," said the sharp-eared chancellor.

"What about letting the bathwater overflow?" piped up one juror.

"That was not a crime," said the chancellor, "but a simple human mistake, for which the palace was amply insured."

"But what about breaking Rupert's crown?" another juror asked.

"Only the foredragon should be talking," said the chancellor. "These cheap crowns they make these days don't last more than a few weeks. Peter has already served enough time in the dungeon to repay *that* debt to society."

"But he *must* be guilty of something!" insisted the foredragon. "What about being in conspiracy with Meredith?"

The chancellor's patience was wearing thin. Still, he consulted the list of charges against Peter. "I don't see anything here about conspiracy," he said. "Who wrote up these charges?"

"Uh—I did, Your Honor." Marcus meekly held up his hand.

"I see," said the chancellor. "Are you legally trained? Never mind, I know the answer. Since Peter was not being charged with conspiracy, he cannot be tried or convicted of conspiracy. Incidentally, this Court is unaware of the existence of any evidence that would support a charge of conspiracy."

To Peter, he said, "My boy, you are free to go; go at once for your own sake, quickly! Leave this land at once; for, clearly, there are many here who wish you harm. After all, as the son of a traitor—"

"—My father was not a traitor!" Peter burst out, without thinking. "He loves this land and wants its wealth to be shared equally by all who dwell here—dragons and humans alike!"

A horrified gasp went up from the jury at the suggestion that this "traitor" could still be alive, for he was thought to be dead. The chancellor's eyes grew stern. But all he said was, "Young man, not another word, or I'll hold you in contempt of court."

"What does that mean?" Peter whispered hoarsely to Marcus, who, as his guard, had come up beside him to escort him out. The shocked dragon jurors murmured in disapproval.

"Silence!" The chancellor banged his gavel loudly.

"I only asked—" said Peter.

Puffs of angry steam and smoke were starting to come from the dragon chancellor's ears. This was not a good sign.

"Marcus, please remove young Peter from this courtroom *now*," said the chancellor calmly. "He does not seem to appreciate that, when a judge calls for silence, he means silence! Let us hope you never find yourself a defendant in a courtroom again, Peter; but if you do, next time, remember that a courtroom is a place for order. There is a time to speak and a time for silence. If you disobey the judge, you risk having the judge find you in contempt. There can be dire consequences if you are held in contempt."

"Like what?" Peter persisted, somehow failing to understand that the judge was giving him a warning.

Marcus was beside himself. *What was wrong with the boy?*

"Come *on*, Peter," urged the worried Marcus, tugging on his sleeve. "Let's go!"

"Get him out of here!" roared the chancellor. "Ahem. I mean, Marcus, please escort young Peter from the courtroom. This case is closed. On to the next case!"

"But—but—where are we going?" Peter said to Marcus who had ahold of him by the elbow. "I can't just leave Meredith without saying goodbye."

"I'll tell her for you," Marcus whispered as he hastily guided Peter out of the courtroom.

As they were heading down the steps, Marcus suddenly remembered something.

"Peter," he said quietly, "your backpack—the one that Rupert's guards took from you when you first got here—I know where it is. Wait here and I'll get it." He dashed back into the building and soon returned with Peter's backpack.

"Thank you, Marcus," said Peter. The other dragon guards were standing around looking bored. They had no reason to distrust Marcus, for they considered him to be "one of them."

"Don't mention it," said Marcus tersely. "You'd better go, now."

"Just a second," said Peter. "I need to give you something from it." He turned away from the others, quickly unzipped his backpack, found the message for Meredith in a secret compartment, and stealthily handed it to Marcus.

"What's this?" Marcus whispered.

"It's for Meredith. Please see that she gets it, and *don't read it!*" Peter whispered back.

The guards were still chattering idly amongst themselves.

Marcus shifted his feet uneasily. "I'll—uh—do my best."

As the iron gates clanged shut behind him, Peter kicked the dirt in frustration.

I'll come back for you as soon as I can, Meredith. I promise, he vowed.

CHAPTER SEVENTEEN

The Silent Stone Walls

In her quiet cell, Meredith lost track of time. When Peter had not returned, she had thought Felix would come and tell her the results of his trial. The more time passed, the greater her apprehensions grew.

It was wintertime, and the days were shorter. There was noticeably less light coming into her dungeon window. She sat on her stone bench, taking small comfort in the snow as it fell silently from the gray skies above.

She had little to do in the dungeon. She had no books to read, for Rupert thought them unnecessary. As a girl growing up in Almira, she had enjoyed learning many ballads, poems, and stories. It comforted her now to sing or recite them to herself. She had learned many of them at her stepmother Esmerelda's knee. Others she had learned from her natural dragon mother, Adella, when she was very small. The few memories she had of Adella were extremely precious to her.

One old ballad—which King Bertram had forbidden to be sung when he was alive—told how his wife, Queen Adella, had mysteriously disappeared one day, never to be seen again. It had been a terrible tragedy. The entire kingdom had mourned her loss.

The song told how one stormy day Queen Adella, Meredith's beautiful young mother, had gone for a walk along the coastline and never returned. No one knew what had happened to her. It was as if the sea had simply swallowed her up. Perhaps she had gotten caught in a tide or been kidnapped by pirate dragons. Perhaps she had hit her head and suffered amnesia, a loss of memory about her past identity that made it impossible for her to find her way home. There were many theories but no real answers.

It was presumed, though, after a reasonable time had passed (seven years), that Adella would not be returning to Deweydaire.

King Bertram had been inconsolable. But then, he had fallen in love with the feisty Esmerelda and asked her to marry him. She had been a good wife to him and a good stepmother to Meredith. She had tried to help Bertram and Meredith forget their sadness and learn to be happy again. Often, she had brought in musicians, actors, and court jesters—like Felix—to entertain them. At long last, joy had returned to Almira Palace.

But then one day, just as Meredith was blossoming into a young dragon beauty (fourteen if translated into human years), Bertram's frail old heart had simply given out. It had come as a terrible shock. Dr. Fitzhugh had tried everything, but he had not been able to save him. Esmerelda and Meredith were left all alone. That was when Dr. Fitzhugh had moved his office into the Palace. He had been there ever since.

Ordinarily, Meredith did not think of these things; but in the dungeon, she had nothing else to do *but* think. Lately, she'd found herself wondering whether her fight for the freedom of others had been worth it, since it had cost her her own. *Not only her freedom but her looks as well*, she thought ruefully, examining her battle-scars. Her face felt grimy. There was never as much water for bathing in the dungeon as she would have liked. She was sure she must look a fright! She was almost glad she had no mirror.

Especially not a mirror into her soul. For Meredith had a nagging feeling she was not entirely innocent. True, she had followed the dictates of her conscience in openly opposing King Harold, but she knew she had gone further than that. She had actively encouraged the human farmers to disobey his laws and refuse to pay the taxes he imposed. Worse, she was the one in charge when the "Fire Chief" had attacked Guldavia—even though he had acted against her orders. In the eyes of Guldavian law, she was responsible for his actions.

Yes, she had been fighting for what she believed: fair treatment for the human farmers. But, in doing so, she had broken King Harold's edicts. She might have been able to work out a truce with Harold—but with Rupert? Such a thing would never have been possible. She almost welcomed her trial, so that she could accept her punishment—whatever it might be—gracefully and regain her peace of mind.

Her troubled thoughts kept her awake long into the night. When she finally did sleep, she dreamed she was back at Almira Palace, dancing at a ball held in her honor. She was the prettiest dragon maiden there! She twirled about on the dance floor with one admiring dragon suitor after another. But, of course, it was all just a dream.

CHAPTER EIGHTEEN

"The Best Oatmeal Cookies"

It was past noon when Meredith was awakened by the sound of tinkling hat-bells on the stairs: Felix! Finally, she would have some news about Peter! She rushed to greet him.

"Felix! Where've you been? What's happened to Peter?"

"Careful—watch out for the tray!" cried Felix. "You'll knock over your lunch. You've slept late. I had a tough time convincing a guard to let me bring you a tray so late in the day. Sit down and I'll hand it to you."

"Thank you, Felix." Meredith sat on the stone ledge that ran against one wall. She could barely wait to hear the news. "Is Peter all right?"

"He's been released," said Felix. "I wanted to come and tell you sooner, but Rupert wouldn't let me." He plopped down on the floor, took out a deck of cards and began to play a game of Solitaire, while she crunched into a stalk of celery spread with cream cheese (something she had never tried before).

"How wonderful for him," Meredith said with a wistful look.

Felix was engrossed in laying out his cards in order in front of him and said nothing. Finally, Meredith could stand the silence no longer.

"It's nice to have your company," she hinted.

He was counting his cards. "One—two—three—did you say something?"

"I was trying to make conversation."

"Oh. Mind if I lay these cards out first?"

Meredith waited as long as she could, then tried again, this time getting right to the point. "Felix, something's been bothering me. You're not a prisoner. You could go home any time you wanted to. Why do you stay here serving such an unworthy prince?"

Felix put down his cards. He had lost his game of *Solitaire* even before he had begun. He sighed, looked up at Meredith, and said, "I would love to go home, dear lady, but that's not so easily done. I can't just up and leave. Here, I have security: a roof over my head, three square meals a day, and a steady job. If I went back to Almira, I'd be starting all over, and all I know how to do is make people laugh. And besides—I hate to say this, but— maybe I'm not even all that funny."

"Well, there are different kinds of humor," said Meredith gently. "Tell me, Felix, don't you have any dreams?"

"Oh, sure," Felix said easily. "I dream every night."

"I'm not talking about ordinary dreams." Meredith gave a faint smile. "Didn't you ever want to do something grand or make something that would last? To leave your mark on the world?"

"Oh, you mean *those* kinds of dreams. Sure, everybody has *those.*"

"Well, Felix, I'm glad to hear you have some ambition beyond just wanting to play the fool here in a fool's court. Don't look so wide-eyed at me, Felix. I know you're no dummy. And I'm counting on you to get me out of here. You're the only hope I've got."

"What do you want me to do, Meredith?" Felix was shuffling his cards uneasily, avoiding her gaze.

"I want you to escort me back to Almira, for which I assure you, you'll be richly rewarded. You'll have everything there that you have here, and more—not only a roof over your head, but a choice position as head jester at Almira Palace."

"But—I can't go back to that job!" Felix wailed, springing to his feet in dismay.

"Why not?"

"Because I was—fired—for not making your father laugh. In those days, that was not such an easy thing to do. Back when I was a young jester-in-training. I told the king a joke he didn't like. It was a 'dragon' joke, one I'd heard the humans tell."

"One of those awful jokes! What was it?"

Felix sighed. "Why do the dragons breathe fire?"

"Why?"

"Indigestion. You see, it's not that funny, or maybe your father had already heard it. I notice you didn't laugh. He didn't either—not that he laughed much in those days—especially at himself—oops! Sorry."

"Maybe your joke gave him indigestion," Meredith observed drily.

"Of course," Felix continued, lost in his thoughts, "only the day before I'd crashed my unicycle into his favorite statue, a bust—terrible timing. A busted bust—get it? *Ha! ha!* Never mind. Anyway, the next day I found myself served with a pink slip and banished from Almira."

Meredith put her scaly hands on his shoulders and looked him squarely in the eye. "Felix, listen to me: none of what you've told me makes one bit of difference! You are my only hope. If you refuse to help me escape on such silly grounds, I shall just—just—cry." This she proceeded to do, loudly and stormily.

"Be still, Meredith, you'll have the guards down here," said Felix in alarm, to which she responded with an even-louder, siren-like wail.

"Meredith, you know very well that if Rupert caught us trying to escape, he'd *never let us live it down*," said Felix, emphasizing his meaning with a slashing gesture under his chin. Meredith flung herself down on her straw bed, crying more loudly than ever, her tears hot on her face.

"Meredith, please try to understand. I'd like to help you, but— you probably didn't know this, but I'm actually a bit of a coward." Another siren-like wail drowned out his feeble pitch.

It was no use. "All right, Meredith, I'm going now." He gathered up her tray of empty dishes and started up the stairs.

She did not stop crying until her throat hurt and she had run out of tears. *Oh, why had she ever come here?* At the time, it had seemed like the only way to stop the fighting between the Red and White Dragons. If only King Harold had been alive when she'd arrived! Things might have worked out so differently! But now, she had to face the stark reality of her situation: she might never escape.

She could certainly never climb out that one small window in her cell. It was too high and small. Even if she could reach it, she would probably get stuck if she tried. Like many Deweydaire dragons, she was somewhat pear-shaped. It would be so humiliating if she got stuck! How Rupert would laugh at her! She could not bear the thought.

Felix had climbed the dungeon stairs and was just getting ready to bang on the door to let the guards know he was ready to leave when it flew open. There stood two guards.

"There you are, Felix," said one of them. "Rupert's been looking everywhere for you." They brushed right past him. Holding the door open with his scaly foot, Felix waited on the stairs, eavesdropping, while they addressed Meredith in gruff unison.

"Our orders are to bring you before Rupert."

"But why?" Felix heard her say. "What about my trial?"

"Just come along with us."

Felix sprang into action. Dashing at top speed to Rupert's throne room, he began to busy himself with a new trick: juggling Meredith's empty dishes while riding his unicycle around and around the outer perimeter of the room, close to the walls.

Rupert's new Chief Advisor (C-A, or, "CA") sat to the left of his throne. The CA frowned sternly at Felix as he cycled past while juggling. No one else—not even Rupert—paid Felix any attention. That is, no one paid him any attention except for Marcus who sat near the throne, his notebook and pencil ready to take notes on the proceedings. He winked conspiratorially at Felix as the jester rode by.

Roughly, the guards led Meredith in before Rupert.

"Sit down, Meredith," Rupert ordered. He reached up to straighten his new crown. This one was tall and heavily laden with jewels. He kept having to adjust it, as it was too big for him. It constantly tilted to one side.

"Thanks, I'd rather stand, cousin." Being a princess, she regarded herself as his equal.

Rupert's face reddened with anger, and puffs of smoke came out his ears. A few of the dragon onlookers snickered, but Meredith remained serene.

"As you wish, then," said Rupert. "Stand!"

Meredith curtsied with exaggerated graciousness.

The CA rose without smiling, cleared his throat, and addressed her.

"Meredith, you were banished from Guldavia for speaking out loudly against King Harold's new laws, but you did not leave. Instead, you hid out with your band of rebel dragons in the hills of Guldavia. Your band wreaked havoc by burning down Guldavia Palace, and—we suspect—committing other acts of destruction as well. You've been nothing but trouble, speaking out on matters which do not concern you. You don't even act like a dragon, although you are one physically. In spirit you are human, which is not a compliment."

"Just because I stand up for the humans doesn't make me a human!" Meredith said defiantly, her eyes blazing at him. "By the way, suspecting is not the same as proving."

"Silence!" the CA roared. "But that's your trouble. You don't know when to keep quiet. You and that friend of yours, that human Peter Porter, seem to have the same problem. Well, we're going to see to it that your trouble-making abilities are *suitably rewarded.*" He smirked sarcastically. "Why, we've even made plans to present you with a special statue in your honor."

"How kind," said Meredith warily.

"Yes. Once you have your statue, you will be free to leave; indeed, we'll even assist you in getting as far away from here as possible."

"Oh really," said Meredith. "What's the catch?"

The CA smirked. "Only that you'll be inside the statue. Oh, don't worry; with any luck, your new home will be quite charming. By magic you will be shrunk and trapped within it. There you will stay, like a genie in a bottle, never to be seen or heard from again!"

Meredith could not believe her ears. This was worse than any fate she could ever have imagined!

"You can't do that!" she cried. "No one has been turned into a statue here for hundreds of years. It can only be done by magic, and that kind of magic is illegal, as you well know! Besides, aren't you getting ahead of yourself? What about my trial? You know the law here: a dragon is innocent until proven guilty. All the laws matter, not just the ones that suit you."

Rupert snickered. "With all the evidence we've got on you, why waste time on a trial? Let's move right into the sentencing hearing. Right, guys?" He looked to his panel of advisors for confirmation. They smiled smirky dragon smiles and nodded in agreement.

"But this is an outrage!" cried Meredith. "You can't just skip the trial. Just wait until Francis the Chancellor hears about this!"

"He won't, until it's too late." Rupert's smile was smug.

"What do you mean by that?" she demanded.

"Oh, just that he's gone away—on a little vacation," said Rupert.

"But he just got back from one!" said Meredith. Then the horrible realization sunk in: "You've done something to him, haven't you."

"How should I know he'd get himself locked in the Tower?" Rupert said. "Although, it serves him right for letting Peter go free."

The Tower! Rupert had imprisoned the chancellor in the Tower of Rhapsody Castle!

Meredith tried to stay calm and think. Her prospects did not look good. There was no proper judge in this proceeding, and she did not have a lawyer. Peter had not had one, either; but at least he had had a trial!

"But, without a trial," she protested, "how will I know what the charges are against me? Am I being charged with conspiracy related to my rebel forces' burning down of Guldavia? Or with exercising my right to free speech? At least tell me what the charges are, so I can defend myself against them."

Rupert looked at the CA. Then they both said, at the same time, "It's a combination of things."

Two guards advanced towards Meredith menacingly.

She stalled for time. "Wait!" she said. "At least I don't steal other people's mail!"

"What? Hold on, guards!" Rupert held up his hand. "Are you accusing me of something, Meredith?" He stepped down from his throne and walked towards her belligerently, ignoring the CA who tried to stop him.

"You heard me." She held her ground.

"You'd better explain before I—I—" Rupert sputtered.

"Certainly," said Meredith. "Peter told me he came here with an important message for me from Almira Palace. What have you done with it, Rupert? Don't you know it's a serious offense to interfere with the royal mail?"

Rupert looked nervous. "Meredith, I knew nothing of this. It must be Marcus's fault."

"Peter told me he thought the message was still in his backpack," said Meredith, with as much righteous indignation as she could muster.

"Somebody fetch that backpack!" No one moved. "Marcus!"

"Here I am, sire." Marcus came dashing up, his ever-present notebook sticking rakishly out of his pocket.

"Marcus, find that backpack."

"What backpack?" Marcus asked with an innocent expression.

"Peter's, you dodo!"

Marcus stifled an angry growl. "But, Your Highness," Marcus informed him sweetly, "I gave Peter back his backpack."

"You *what*?"

"I think that just about wraps things up." The CA crossed his arms smugly.

"Guards! Arrest Marcus!" cried Rupert.

"Wait!" Marcus reconsidered. "Let me think …. There *may* have been such an envelope. If so, it'd be back in my room. Yes, I believe I did see such an envelope."

"Well, go get it," roared Rupert.

Everyone waited for what seemed like hours. Finally, the CA rose, declaring, "Your Highness, let's stop this charade. There is no evidence—"

Just then Marcus dashed in, holding the envelope with Dr. Fitzhugh's message to Meredith inside. He hoped no one would notice that "someone" had broken the seal.

"Here it is, sire," he said, all out of breath. "Would you like me to—uh—open it and read it to you?"

Meredith cleared her throat loudly. "I believe that's my letter," she said, holding out her taloned hand for it.

Rupert waved her aside. "Go ahead, Marcus."

Marcus, with an apologetic look at Meredith, unfolded the paper "dragon" and read:

> Dear Meredith:
>
> Your mother is ill. She has revealed under hypnosis that she is sorry she wasn't nice to you and is heartsick for your return. Then she fell into a deep sleep. The trouble is, she won't wake up! No, she is not pretending. Please, won't you come home as soon as you can?
>
> Sincerely,
> Dr. George Fitzhugh, Chief Palace Physician
> Almira Palace

Rupert's expression softened as Marcus read. His reptilian eyes looked moist. "Poor Aunt Esmerelda," he murmured. "She always did bake the best oatmeal cookies."

Meredith seized her opportunity. "Rupert," said Meredith, "as a last request, please! Let me go to Esmerelda. She needs me! You can trust me to return, after I have done what I can for her."

Rupert looked as if he were about to say "yes" when he was suddenly rushed upon by all four advisors, who huddled about him, murmuring in his ear.

Meredith could only hear snatches: "No, Your Highness—it's a trick," and, "She'll never return if you let her leave!"

Rupert gave the order: "Guards, take her away!"

"Why, Rupert? We're cousins. Don't listen to *them*." Meredith pointed at the advisors who scowled back at her. "Remember when we used to make mud pies together when we were small— even if you did try to make me eat them? I forgave you for that then. Can't you forgive me now?"

"Guards!" shouted Rupert. "Why don't you come when I call you!"

Two guards came reluctantly towards her. "No, no, you can't," she cried desperately, but it was no use. They had their orders. She did not see two other guards who came sneaking up behind her. They placed a wet cloth with a sickly-sweet smell over her mouth and nose. Soon she was out cold.

"That's it! That's it!" the four advisors cried, clapping their hands with glee as the guards dragged Meredith away. "We'll trap her in a statue and send her far away. No one will know who she is, and we'll have no more rebellions to quash! She'll never be seen or heard from again!"

CHAPTER NINETEEN

Double-Dealing

Felix was aghast. He had witnessed the whole "trial" while juggling and riding his unicycle around and around the perimeter of the "courtroom" (Rupert's throne room). *How could Rupert do such a thing to Meredith?* She didn't deserve this! Wasn't there some way she could escape this horrible fate? He could think of only one person brave enough to help: Peter Porter. Certainly not himself!

He must let Peter know as soon as possible that Meredith's situation had gone from bad to terrible. Forgetting to be a coward, he did something truly brave. While no one was looking, he made a quick exit on his unicycle out an open side door of Rupert's throne room, bounced down ten steps to the ground, and set out for the Porter farm. No one stopped or questioned him, for he was thought to be a harmless fool.

He pedaled furiously down the road towards Almira, looking for signs that might give him some idea where the Porter farm was. He did not see a single sign. Once, when he stopped to ask directions, a farmer told him: "Take this road for about four miles, then turn right." The trouble was, Felix didn't know how to tell when he had gone four miles. There were no markers on the road, and odometers for unicycles did not yet exist. The time was short. He could not afford to get lost or stay lost for long. He was sure he must have gone four miles by now, but he had not seen any crossroads. Figuring he must have missed the turn, he turned around, or "backtracked."

It was in the confusion of changing course that he almost ran into a mysterious old foot traveler who seemed to appear out of nowhere. He was wearing a long, tattered gray robe, tied with a sash of twisted white cord. He carried a walking stick. After Felix made his apologies, the two fell into pleasant conversation.

"I've always been terrible at directions," Felix admitted.

"If you keep on this way, you'll end up in Elmira, New York instead of Almira, Deweydaire," the old fellow joked. "Don't ask me to explain; you'd never understand. Why are you in such a hurry, anyway?"

Felix found himself telling the man about Meredith, the danger she was in, and how he hoped to recruit Peter to rescue her. The traveler drew a map for Felix. He also gave him clear directions to the Porter Farm. He explained that the turn-off was an easy one to miss, if you didn't know what you were looking for. It was an unmarked side road that went only to the right. That road would take you down a long, winding lane that ended at the Porter farm. It was easy to miss the turn-off, the man explained, for wild rosebushes had grown up, obscuring the view. Yes, the Porter Farm was very hard to find, if you did not know exactly what you were looking for.

Before they parted as fast friends, the mysterious traveler gave Felix the following advice: "Try to make a 'mental picture' of this crossroads in your mind. That will help you find your way back when it's time.

"Now," he continued, "I have a riddle for you and Peter. I suggest you learn it 'by heart' or write it down." Slowly, he recited to Felix the following riddle poem:

Searcher, truth I would not feign,
What you seek, don't seek in vain.
If you use both brawn and brain,
You'll see the mountain, cleft in twain.
(You may also have to take a train.)

"But what does it mean?" asked Felix. "*Cleft in twain? Take a train?* I have never heard of a *train* (There were no trains in Deweydaire). Will I ever see you again? Will you tell me your name?"

"You're asking too many questions," said the mysterious traveler, with a laugh that showed gaps where he was missing several teeth. "You and Peter need to figure this out on your own. You can do it. Goodbye, now, and good luck. Persistence is the key. Never give up." Then, with an encouraging wink and a wave of his walking stick, he disappeared down the road.

Pondering the riddle, Felix pedaled steadily, now in the right direction, towards the Porter farm.

* * *

Meanwhile, back at Rhapsody Palace, Rupert and his advisors had already begun to put their dastardly plan into action.

There was rumored to be only one magician left in the land who knew how to turn dragons into statues. His name was Carlos Giordano. He kept to himself, living in a tiny hut at the edge of the Guldavian Forest with his little black-and-white dog, Ferdie who was part-Deweydaire Terrier and part-Guldavian Border Collie. Now, Ferdie was a smart little dog with a long, swishy tail. He minded pretty well, except when he "forgot to."

Now, Carlos was an old man, but he was still a fine artist. He was a wood sculptor who made clocks, statues, and other beautiful things out of wood.

After a long day of traipsing through the forest, looking for just the right tree, and then chopping it down, Carlos was relaxing in a comfy chair, soaking his sore feet in a tub of hot water. He was still wearing his brown leather work apron. He had a patchwork quilt over his lap. A melted cheese sandwich and bowl of steaming tomato soup waited for him on the small table next to his chair, along with a copy of his favorite novel, *Pinocchio*. Ferdie was curled up at his feet on a colorful braided rag rug. A cozy fire blazed in the fireplace.

Suddenly, Ferdie's ears perked up. "*Grr*," he growled, low in his throat.

A loud rapping at the door was heard.

"Who is it!" Carlos called out, without getting up.

"It's Prince Rupert. Open up!"

"Just a second." The stooped, white-haired woodcarver slowly rose to his feet and went to the door.

"Hello, Carlos," said Rupert, barging his way past Carlos into his hut. "I know your secret." Marcus trailed behind him, prepared to take notes or otherwise make himself useful.

"What are you talking about? I don't have a secret." Carlos's eyes were wide with innocence under his shaggy white eyebrows.

Rupert began snooping around. "Don't think you can hide the fact that you're a magician from me. What's in this chest here? Your tools of the trade, no doubt."

"Don't open that!" cried Carlos. "Uh—it hasn't been opened in a long time, and you don't want to have to breathe in that awful smell. Mothballs, you know."

Rupert considered, then drew his scaly hand back. "I've heard the rumors about you. It's said you make magic clocks that have hands like human hands and *very interesting* statues."

"So what if I do make clocks," said Carlos. "There's no magic involved in that. You've got me all wrong. I'm just a lowly woodcarver, carving my clocks—and an occasional statue—and selling them for a pittance."

"There's no need to pretend, Carlos. But don't worry; your secret is safe with me—just as long as you do what I ask."

"And what would that be?" Carlos asked warily.

"Aha! So, you *admit* you're a magician!"

"Laying traps, that's what you do," muttered Carlos.

"So! you don't deny it!" said Rupert smugly. He turned toward Marcus and said, "Write that down, Marcus."

He already had done so.

"Now, Carlos," said Rupert, "You're an old man, *aren't* you."

Ferdie snarled at Rupert, bristling as if to say, I *smell a rat*.

"Ferdie, quiet!" Carlos said to his dog. "My age is none of your business. What is it you want, Rupert?"

Rupert whispered into Carlos's ear: Psst.

Carlos frowned at him. "But turning a princess into a statue is not something one does lightly! What if her father found out? Why, he'd be furious with me!"

"Don't worry! Her father is dead, and her stepmother, who happens to be my aunt, has fallen into a fairy-tale sleep. *Snow White's Syndrome*, I think they call it. She's pretty feisty, but she's not likely to wake up anytime soon."

"*Snow White's Syndrome*, eh. I've heard of that," said Carlos. "Even so, I'm not interested. I've given up the practice of magic."

"You're a tough negotiator, Carlos," said Rupert. "What would it take to change your mind. I'll give you anything you want—well, just about anything."

"I'm *not interested!*" said Carlos. "My supper's getting cold, so...."

"I'll come back tomorrow for your final answer," said Rupert. "Come on, Marcus."

"Don't slam the—"

Rupert slammed the door. It rattled, loose on its hinges.

The next day, Rupert returned. "I trust you've come to your senses, Carlos?"

"I haven't changed my mind, if that's what you mean," said Carlos. "You're the last dragon I'd ever make a deal with."

"What do you mean by that!" Rupert demanded.

"There are a lot of reasons," said Carlos. "For one, my dog doesn't like you."

"Heh heh. Come here, nice puppy!"

Ferdie growled and stayed put.

"Heh heh. Now Carlos, let's be reasonable. What would you like in exchange? A bag of gold coins? A new hut?"

"What I want most, you'd never give me," said Carlos.

"What's that?" asked Rupert.

"Permission to leave Deweydaire," said Carlos.

"That's impossible," said Rupert. "No one is allowed to leave Deweydaire. You know the rules."

"Sometimes there are exceptions to the rules," suggested Carlos with a wistful smile. "I'd be willing to test the boundaries of what is possible.

"Have you ever heard of Philadelphia? It's said to be 'the birthplace of modern liberty.' A place where human freedom is cherished so much that men have been willing to fight and die for it. I am not sure if it is a real place or just an ideal, but I'd like to try and find it. I'd gladly spend my last days there."

"Philadelphia, huh. 'Never heard of it," said Rupert.

"No, *you* wouldn't have," Carlos muttered.

"And just what do you mean by that?" Rupert demanded, placing his hands on his hips belligerently.

"Uh—well—how would you have?" Carlos said quickly. "You probably didn't know that the word *Philadelphia* means 'brotherly love,' either, did you? It comes from the Greek words *philos* meaning 'love' and *adelphos* meaning 'brother.'"

"Greek, huh. Since when did you ever study Greek?" Rupert scoffed.

"Who says I did?" said Carlos. "You can find that information in the dictionary. Intriguing, isn't it? Actually, I might have studied Greek once, so long ago that I forgot most of it. If I did, it must've been before I made that little mistake in magic that landed me here. Heh heh. That's all 'ancient history' now.

"One thing I do know, Rupert, is that I've lived many years under the cruel rule of the dragons. There is no freedom here. Oh, the written law would be fair, if it were enforced as it is written. But no. Instead, the ruler makes the law up as he goes along. Why, a magician can't even practice magic here without royal permission!"

Rupert blinked. "My father wasn't such a bad ruler!"

"No," agreed Carlos. "He wasn't."

Angry puffs of smoke came out of Rupert's ears. "Are you saying I'm a bad ruler?"

"If the shoe fits," said Carlos, shrugging his shoulders. "Did you know the first 'ruler' was the same length as a king's foot—twelve inches?"

"Stop changing the subject!" cried Rupert.

"It's not the *subject* I'd like to change," Carlos muttered, half under his breath.

"What did you say, Carlos?" said Rupert, taking a menacing step towards Carlos.

"Remember, I'm the last remaining magician in the land," said Carlos smugly, taking a step backwards. "I don't think you can afford to argue with me."

"*Hmpf!* Well, at least you didn't ask for Meredith's freedom, or for favors for those precious human farmers of hers. I admire a man who knows how to take care of himself. All right, you can go. Go find this place called Philadelphia that's so important to you—on one condition: you must take Meredith with you. Just remember, though, that once you leave Deweydaire, you can never, never return."

"So they say," muttered Carlos. "I wouldn't want to, anyway."

"If you go, you go at your own risk."

"I accept that."

"Good. Are we going to shake on this or aren't we," Rupert demanded. He thrust his cold, scaly hand toward Carlos.

Carlos hesitated. If only there were some other way for him to leave Deweydaire!

"It's settled, then." Rupert squeezed Carlos's hand hard.

"All right, Rupert," said Carlos, rubbing his sore hand. "Bring your dragon princess to me. And stop crossing your fingers behind your back."

"I will when you stop crossing yours!" Rupert called over his shoulder as he headed out the door. Ferdie snarled: *good riddance!*

* * *

Meredith, however, refused to cooperate with Rupert's plan. She stopped eating her daily ration of oatmeal or anything else. Before long, she had grown pale and sickly. Even Rupert could see that she was too weak to travel.

Exasperated, Rupert ordered Carlos to report to the Rhapsody dungeon for artist duty at once. However, Carlos did not like that plan—not at all.

"I'm an artist," Carlos pleaded to Rupert. "I can't work in that dungeon! It's dark and dingy. I need light, northern light, to do my best work."

"That's not in your contract," said Rupert.

"Rupert, be reasonable," said Carlos. "You hired me to make you a statue, and I agreed to do it, but I need good northern light to do my best work. I have such light in my hut. On the other hand, the light in your dungeon is terrible. Please, Rupert. Send Meredith to my hut so I can work on the statue of her there."

"You're the one who's not being reasonable," said Rupert bluntly. "As I've already told you, the answer is no. Meredith is too weak to travel. Period."

"But—." Carlos looked around the throne room. Mean-looking guards stood at every exit. They looked as if they would be more than happy to grab him the moment Rupert gave them the okay.

"Well, heh heh, I guess I could start out in the dungeon, just to make a few sketches," said Carlos.

So, Carlos had carried his box full of art supplies to the dungeon. After he had drawn five or six preliminary pencil sketches, he showed them to Meredith.

"Which one do you like best?" he asked.

"None of them," said Meredith. "Your work is excellent, but I am not playing this game. I refuse to cooperate with a scheme that will result in my own imprisonment."

"Fair enough," said Carlos. "I'll pick one." He chose his favorite. As it happened, it was Meredith's favorite, too.

As Carlos began the actual carving of the statue, she began to grow more interested. After all, there was something immensely flattering, she thought, about having someone carve your likeness in wood.

"Say, Carlos."

"Yes?"

"I was just wondering how you were going to make the eyes look real."

"What do you mean?" asked Carlos, carefully chipping away at the wood with a chisel. "Whoops! I made a little mistake, but I can fix it so it will look even better than before."

"You could put in pretty gemstones for the eyes," Meredith suggested. "I was thinking maybe you could use those stones they call 'dragon's eyes.' They are red, with dark stripes running through them. They are like 'tiger's eyes,' but more red than gold. I think those would be perfect, don't you?"

"I suppose," said Carlos absent-mindedly as he chiseled away, "if I can find them."

"Well, would you at least try to look for them?" asked Meredith.

"I'll see what I can do," he said. "Now, Meredith, won't you come back with me to my hut where there's better light? Don't you want to get out of this dungeon? I know I do!"

Weak as she was from her hunger strike, and against her better judgment, Meredith agreed.

"I'll come with you on one condition," she said. "Promise you will use 'dragon's eyes' for the statue's eyes."

"Sure, anything you say!" said Carlos. "Just let's get out of this dungeon!"

Rupert, however, was not taking any chances. He had Meredith transported to Carlos's hut in chains, accompanied by a great many guards. As if she had the strength to escape!

Carlos was glad to be back in his own little hut. He set right to work carving the statue.

Twice, Rupert came by to check on his progress, but Carlos refused to see him. He barred the door by piling furniture against it. "Go away!" he told Rupert. "I must have solitude to do my best work."

After Carlos had spent many long days stretching into the night chipping away at the statue with his carving tools, he laid down his chisel for the last time.

"Isn't it magnificent, Ferdie!" he said, yawning and stretching as dawn arose. "And to think that I started out with a block of mere wood!"

There on the kitchen table sat his masterpiece. It was about twelve inches high and a little wider, due to its outstretched-wings. Knotty horns sprouted from its high forehead of dark, polished mahogany. The sleek body curved gracefully. Every line was smooth and elegant. There was not a single flaw (at least, not one that was obvious).

"It's dragon perfection," said Carlos, beaming.

Ferdie whined insistently and walked in circles.

"What's wrong, boy? Do you have to go out? No? Hey, calm down .... What are you trying to tell me?" He put his hands on his hips and stared at Ferdie who looked deeply into his eyes.

"I forgot about those 'dragon's eyes,' didn't I, Ferdie?" said Carlos, feeling guilty.

Ferdie sat down, satisfied, having made his point.

"Well, there's no time to go looking for them now," said Carlos. "Rupert didn't give me much time, and he didn't give me an expense account, either. Now, I do have a pair of old cufflinks that are set with light-green peridot that I could take apart. They ought to make gorgeous eyes for Meredith. I bet she's forgotten all about the 'dragon's eyes.' She probably won't even notice the difference."

Ferdie seemed to disagree. He put his paws up on Carlos's legs and tried to get his attention, but Carlos ignored him. The woodcarver rummaged in his dresser drawer and found the cufflinks.

"I hate to ruin these cufflinks, but it's for my art," he told Ferdie as he pried them loose. "Meredith ought to be able to see through these just fine, after I add my magic touch." He soon had the light-green peridot gemstones set in place in the statue's empty eye sockets.

"There! *Now* what do you think, Ferdie?" said Carlos.

Ferdie began to pace in worried circles again.

"Let's put it here where she can see it as soon as she wakes up. I can't wait to get her reaction, can you, boy?"

Ferdie trotted over to the straw bedding where Meredith slept to nudge her awake. "Carlos, I think Ferdie needs to go out," said Meredith. "Hey, Ferdie, knock it off!" Ferdie was licking her face enthusiastically.

"Good morning, Bright Eyes," Carlos said cheerfully. "At last, my work is done. I can't wait to show it to you. Are you ready?" He whisked away the white cloth covering the statue with a flourish.

Meredith rubbed the sleep from her eyes and looked at the finished statue for the first time. Then she looked away sadly.

"What's wrong?" asked Carlos. "Don't you like it?"

"Oh Carlos!" said Meredith. "It is a lovely statue, but how do you really expect me to feel about all this?"

"What do you mean?" asked Carlos.

"You have created a beautiful work of art, but it will be my prison. Incidentally, was there some reason why you did not put clothes on the statue?"

"I knew you were going to bring that up," said Carlos. "Yes. The statue is a work of art. Let me reassure you that dragons in art are not usually depicted wearing clothing."

"Hmm," said Meredith, unconvinced. "There's another problem: you gave the statue horns. *Why* did you make it with horns when—as you can plainly see—I don't have horns?"

"I thought it looked better with horns. Besides, they're just little ones."

"That is not really okay. But what bothers me the most, Carlos—and I think you know what I'm going to say—is that you *promised* you'd use 'dragon's eyes' for the eyes. It was the one condition I insisted upon before I agreed to cooperate. And it's clear that you have used some other kind of stone."

Carlos tried to explain. "Yes, I used green peridot. Meredith, I didn't *intentionally* renege on my promise. I didn't think it would matter all that much what kind of stones I used, as long as they were pretty. As an artist, don't I have the freedom to make a statue the way I want to? I didn't have the time or money to go out looking for rare gemstones. I used what I had. Now tell me, honestly: aren't these eyes lovely?"

"No!" said Meredith stubbornly, although she knew they were. They matched the ring her grandfather had given her.

"You were lucky to get jewels at all from a poor woodcarver like me!" said Carlos.

"What made you so generous?" said Meredith sarcastically.

"You don't seem very grateful," said Carlos. "I have worked hard to create a beautiful statue for you. I feel sorry for you, but you've brought a lot of this on yourself."

"Well, that's a mean thing to say!" exclaimed Meredith. "The things I did that got me into trouble, I did to help others. I don't want your pity!"

Then, seeing Carlos's hurt look, she said gently, "The statue is beautiful, Carlos, but—how do you really expect me to feel? Thrilled? I—I'd like to be alone now, please. I think I'm going to cry; in fact, I'm sure of it."

"I—guess I'll go see if Ferdie wants to go out," Carlos mumbled, shuffling off in his slippers.

"Felix—Peter—if you care at all—where are you? Meredith whispered urgently into the night.

CHAPTER TWENTY

To Scale or Not to Scale?

In fact, Felix, on his unicycle, had just that morning arrived, finally, at the Porter farm, tired and disheveled. He had lost his jester's cap of bells somewhere in the Guldavian Hills. All those hills on a unicycle! He was exhausted.

When he knocked timidly at Peter's cottage door, no one answered. He knocked again more loudly. Still, there was no answer. Since he was afraid he'd get lost if he wandered about the farm on his own, he sat down on the front porch steps to wait for Peter. Before he knew it, he had fallen asleep in the hot sun.

"Ma-a-a! Ma-a-a!"

What was that? It sounded like goats! Felix looked up to see Peter trudging up the lane carrying two pails of goats' milk. Two goats trotted along behind him. Felix sprang to his feet.

"Peter!" he cried. "Where have you been?"

"I was working. Why? What's the matter?"

"Meredith is in trouble," said Felix in a rush, "and she needs your help right away! That horrible Rupert is going to shut her up in a wooden statue and send her far away—so far away that she'll never be able to return!"

"What!" Peter stopped fast, splashing milk from the pails. "I always meant to get back to her. Here, Felix, bring these pails to the house for me, will you? I must go to her at once. I'll have to figure out what to do about Mearsie and Dosie, though." He ran towards the house.

"Wait, Peter!" Felix huffed to catch up with him, lugging the milk pails. Peter stopped and waited for him. "Who is going to take care of these goats? Where's your mom?"

"She's been staying with a sick friend in Avonia," said Peter as they walked towards the house together. "I don't know when she'll be back, and I don't have a way to reach her. She's been counting on me to take care of the farm in her absence."

"I guess you can't go, then," said Felix, practically. Then he realized where the conversation was heading. "Oh no," he protested. "Absolutely not."

"Felix, why not?" asked Peter. "You could stay here and tend to the goats and the rest of the farm while I'm gone. That way, you'll be able to explain everything to Mom when she gets back. Just tell her it's about Meredith and that *Dad is involved*. She'll understand."

"I'd like to help, of course; but I don't know anything about goats," said Felix, wringing his taloned hands in a worried way.

"You can do it, Felix," Peter encouraged him. "Just give them food and water, milk them, and clean out their stalls every day. It doesn't hurt to pet them, either, or to 'talk nice' to them, and thank them for their milk. It's all in the farm manual; I'll leave it for you. If you want to try making cheese, be my guest. This is a good plan. This way, when Mom gets back, you'll be right here to explain everything."

"Well, Marcus did say he'd try to cover for me, so Rupert wouldn't get suspicious," said Felix. "He and I do look quite a bit alike."

"You really do," Peter agreed. "So, you'll do it, then? Thanks so much, Felix. Say, while I pack, do you think you could make me a couple of peanut butter and jelly sandwiches for the road?"

"Sure, if I can find the peanut butter." The jester began to open the kitchen cupboards, looking for it.

Peter was just backing down the loft ladder when Felix returned with a bagful of sandwiches and a good-sized chunk of goat cheese.

"You know, Peter," began Felix, "I agree that we must act quickly, but we must also have a plan."

"What sort of plan?" asked Peter, as he slid the toggle button on his backpack into the closed position (zippers having not yet been invented in Deweydaire).

"Well, let's think this through," said Felix. "You can't just head for Rhapsody Castle. Most likely, Rupert's guards will just take you prisoner if you do. Besides, Meredith may not even be there anymore."

"Well, then, where should I go?" Both grew quiet for a few moments, deep in thought.

Then Peter said, "Felix, you said Rupert was going to imprison Meredith in a statue."

"Yes, that's what he said."

"How would he do such a thing, Felix?"

"Beats me. By some sort of magic, I suppose."

"You also said he planned to send her far, far away," Peter continued. "What do you think he means by that? The farthest place away from here that I can think of is Newtesia. Maybe I should head for Newtesia!"

"Not so fast, Peter," said Felix. "I've been giving this matter some serious thought on my way here, while I was pedaling down the road."

"*Serious* thought! Isn't that a lot to ask of a jester?" Peter teased him.

"How can you joke at a time like this!" cried Felix. "We jesters are under-appreciated!"

"Sorry. I do value your opinion, Felix. Walk me to the main

road and tell me all your thoughts on this, okay?"

"Okay," agreed Felix, "but please listen carefully. The time is short, but it is still important to get this right. We may only have one chance to help Meredith." They started down the Porters' lane to the main road.

"So, Felix, you don't think Rupert is planning to send Meredith to Newtesia? Well, where would he send her, then? To Avonia? That's pretty far away, too, but in the opposite direction."

"Peter, I think Rupert has something even more sinister in mind for Meredith," said Felix. "The farthest place I can think of is—no, he wouldn't. Not even Rupert would do that!" Felix shuddered at the vision his imagination had conjured up.

"What, Felix? Please tell me!"

"Peter, the farthest place I can imagine that Rupert could send her to would be ... to the other side of the Deweydaire Mountains."

"Is such a thing even possible?" asked Peter, incredulously.

"Peter, what do you know about the Deweydaire Mountains?"

"Not much. My mom told me never to go near them. She said there was a magic in them that was not well-understood."

"With good reason," said Felix. "We dragons believe that, once anyone crosses those mountains, he can never return. No one ever has—that we know of. We dragons don't normally discuss such things with you humans, but this is an exception—what with your being the only one who can help Meredith and all."

"I'll do all I can," said Peter, "only—how do I do it, Felix? How do I cross those mountains?"

"Oh, Peter! If only it were that easy! You cannot scale them. No one can. There are too many of them, and they are too tall and steep. Plus, they're covered in sheets of black glassy rock. It might be a kind of obsidian, but it's not broken up into boulders, rocks, and rubble like you might have seen on other mountains that people do climb.

"No, the Deweydaire Mountains are the most forbidding mountains you could ever imagine. I don't see how any human could possibly hope to cross them. You might think: oh, anyone could just break up that glassy rock with a pickax as he went along, but no. There's just too much of it. I'm afraid a person would likely not survive the attempt."

"Then why are we even talking about it, Felix?"

"Because ... there might be another way."

"Oh, please! Tell me, Felix! What is this other way?"

Felix hesitated. "First, Peter, please understand. There is no guarantee that, even if you make it to the other side of the mountains, you will be able to return to Deweydaire. If you remain stuck on the other side, you will never see your family again. Are you willing to take that chance? Are you willing to help Meredith and her Cause, even if it means losing everything?"

Now Peter was the one to hesitate. "I don't know. That sounds like a risk no one in his right mind would ever take. Isn't there any other way to help Meredith?"

"I don't think so, Peter. The more I think about it, the more I'm sure that Rupert is planning to banish Meredith from Deweydaire forever," said Felix. "Do you still want to hear about my 'other way,' or have you decided this is too much to ask?"

"Go ahead and tell me," said Peter. "I'll give you my answer after I've heard all the details."

"That's fair. The thing is: maybe the way out is not *over* the mountains but *through* them."

"What do you mean, 'through them'?" asked Peter.

"Dragons believe there are cave corridors within the Deweydaire Mountains that go on for miles and miles. The mountains were once volcanic, and such passages were formed by lava which is molten rock, rock that got so hot it melted. They are sometimes called *lava tubes*. The most fabled of these passages is called Anselm's Way."

"Anselm's Way," Peter repeated. "I've never heard of it."

"No, you wouldn't have. As I've said, we dragons don't usually talk about such things with you humans."

"Was Anselm a dragon?" asked Peter. "Hey, is he the one whose face is on the gold coin you dragons call a *draco*?"

"That's right," said Felix. "He was the dragon founder of Deweydaire who led our ancestors here in flight long, long ago."

In flight! Peter was intrigued. "In flight from what?"

"In flight from St. George and the other dragon-slaying knights," explained Felix patiently. "Deweydaire was our refuge. You probably learned about St. George in school, didn't you?"

"Of course," said Peter. "He's known as the 'soldier's saint.' Soldiers in the heat of battle have claimed he appeared to them in the sky, encouraging them to keep fighting for their Cause. St. George was a real person, a Christian martyr. My history books say he tore down the proclamation of the Roman emperor Diocletian, ordering the persecution of Christians. Other books say he slew a dragon in order to rescue a princess. This happened, I believe, in a swamp in Silene—or was that Cyrene?"

"Berkshire is the way I heard it," said Felix, "and the dragon's name was 'Snap,' but who can know? All of this is all so steeped in myth and legend; it's hard to tell fact from fiction.

"I guess you can see why St. George is not regarded as a hero by dragons! In fact, he was Anselm's worst enemy! Why, St. George and his knights practically wiped out the world's entire dragon population! That was why Anselm led the few surviving dragons here, in flight, and founded Deweydaire, a new civilization, to be ruled by dragons."

"I see," said Peter, realizing he was treading in sensitive, even sacred, territory. Still, he had to ask: "There's something I don't understand. How is Anselm's Way related to Anselm?"

"I don't know, exactly," said Felix. "Maybe Anselm discovered Anselm's Way. Perhaps you will find out. For, if you're going to get to the other side of those mountains, I believe you're going to have to find Anselm's Way."

"Okay. How do I do that, Felix?"

"I'm not sure, but I may have an idea or two. Do you remember when I mentioned meeting a mysterious traveler on the road, on my way here?"

"Yes."

"Well, when I told him about the situation with Meredith, he wanted to help you find her. He taught me a poem, a riddle with clues in it. He said I should teach it to you. May I read it to you."

Felix pulled the poem from his "jester's motley" pants pockets and read it aloud to Peter:

> Searcher, truth I would not feign,
> What you seek, don't seek in vain.
> If you use both brawn and brain,
> You'll see the mountain, cleft in twain.
> (You may also have to take a train.)

"Cleft in twain! Train! What a strange refrain!" said Peter, rhyming unintentionally. "Say, I wonder if music could be involved. In music, 'middle C' separates the high notes of the treble clef from the low notes of the bass clef. It divides the complete range of musical notes into two parts."

"That's right, 'professor,'" joked Felix. "Although in music the word is spelled 'c-l-e-f,' not 'c-l-e-f-t.'"

"Oh, you're right," said Peter. "A cleft chin is one that has a dimple in it—like yours. Sorry. I didn't mean to sound like a know-it-all."

"It's fine," said Felix, touching his chin reflectively. "Now, *twain* means 'twin.' To get two parts, you cleave—which means cut or split—one whole into twain—into two parts. As for *train*, that's a word I've never heard before. I haven't a clue what a *train* is."

"Me either," said Peter. He thought a bit. "Hey, Felix, do you suppose *cleft in twain* could refer to Anselm's Way? In a sense, a passageway that goes all the way through a mountain might be said to 'cleave' or 'divide' it into two parts."

"Peter, you may be on to something," said Felix. "I wish we had more clues, but we don't. Maybe, while you are looking for Meredith, you could keep your eyes open for anything that goes by the name of a *train*. Who knows where your journey might take you? In a way, I envy you, getting to go on such a grand adventure."

"You're welcome to come with me," Peter said. "I'd love to have your company."

"No, someone needs to stay here, remember." Felix thought a bit. "Peter, this may be nothing, but two lines from an old jump-rope rhyme just popped into my head. Don't look so surprised. Yes, I jump rope! We jesters have to stay in training, you know. Now, see whether you think there might be a clue hidden in this rhyme." He recited:

If Anselm's Way you wish to find,
Seek Mt. Maurice! Don't get left behind!

"Okay, you've just explained Anselm's Way to me; but what is Mt. Maurice?" asked Peter.

"It's only the tallest, most forbidding, mountain in the Dewey-daire mountain range," said Felix. "In fact, my grandparents used to call it 'The Great Glass Mountain.'"

"So," said Peter thoughtfully. "If the words in that jump-rope rhyme mean anything, they might be a hint that the entrance to Anselm's Way is located on or near Mt. Maurice. What do you think, Felix?"

"I think you're on the right track, Peter. You're good at finding things. Remember how you found that secret button into Rupert's dungeon."

"That was just luck," said Peter modestly.

"I never had that kind of luck," said Felix. "Peter, you can do this! Promise me, though, that you'll be careful and not take unnecessary risks. I don't want to frighten you, but you will undoubtedly face real dangers on this journey. You really ought not to be going alone. Your mother would have a fit if she knew." Felix wrung his scaly hands in a worried way.

"Are you *sure* you don't want to come with me?" asked Peter.

"In a way I do want to, but I can't. I just can't," said Felix. "Besides, someone has to stay here and take care of the goats until your mom gets back, remember. I'll be with you in spirit, though. Say, would you like to borrow my unicycle? I'd be glad to run back and get it for you."

"No, thank you," said Peter. "How can you ride that thing, anyway?"

"It takes a little practice," said Felix. "I still fall down sometimes. In fact, I slid in some loose gravel on my way here."

"I wondered how you got all skinned up—or should I say, 'scaled up,'" Peter quipped.

"That's me, 'upscale'!" Felix quipped back.

"Now you should sing: Do-re-mi—"

"—fa-so-la-ti-do," Felix sang the notes of the well-known musical scale. Then he sang them in reverse order to these words, "Let's-be-sure-you're-read-y-to-go.

"Okay," he continued, after taking a breath. "I've packed your toothbrush and dental floss, a 'super-sized' package which was all I could find. Oh, and I threw in a bunch of candles and a box of matches."

"Thanks, *Mom*," Peter joked. "Sounds like you've thought of everything. I guess this is it, then."

"Wait, Peter! Look over there, in that tree by the road. There's something dangling from the lowest branch. Let's go see what it is." They walked over to the tree.

"It looks like some sort of hat," said Felix, grabbing hold of the device's chin strap and sliding it off the branch. "Hey, look at this, Peter. It lights up! It's like a lamp for your head—a *head-lamp*! That's clever!" He handed the headlamp to Peter.

"Maybe that mysterious traveler came back and left it for you. He told me he liked to invent new-fangled contraptions. See how easy it is to turn it on-and-off?" Felix showed Peter the on-off switch.

"That'll be great to have, for sure," said Peter, somehow finding room for it in his backpack which was already full.

"If you like, you can borrow my special glow-in-the-dark stone," said Felix. "It gets really bright. It might be nice to have it along as a back-up."

"Can you spare it? Won't you need it when you're riding your unicycle at night?"

"When you get back, you can give it back to me," said Felix. He wore it around his neck, strung on a cord. He took it off and placed it around Peter's neck.

Peter felt encouraged. If Felix weren't expecting to see him again, he never would have let him borrow his special glow-in-the-dark stone.

"You know, Felix, you really are pretty smart, and I don't mean 'just for a jester.'"

The jester flashed his toothy dragon grin. "That sounds like a compliment. Thank you."

They said their goodbyes, and then Peter was off.

* * *

Time was running out, though; for in his Guldavian hut, a lowly woodcarver with shaggy white eyebrows was getting ready to cast a little magic spell.

PART THREE:
JOURNEYS

CHAPTER TWENTY-ONE

"Is That You, Statue?"

W hat are you doing, Carlos?" Meredith asked nervously as the magician closed the curtains. She had known, of course, that her days of freedom would be "numbered," once he had finished carving the statue.

"The time has come," said Carlos. "In honor of the upcoming magic spell I am about to perform, I've composed a little poem. Would you like to hear it?"

"Do I have a choice?" said Meredith.

"I'll take that as a 'yes.'" Carlos struck a dramatic pose and recited:

> Into this statue you must go
> For Rupert commands it so.
> I do this quite reluctantly.
> I'd be glad if you could flee.
> Though you have wings—if I'm not wrong—
> You've never worked to make them strong.
> It seems you've never tried to fly.
> Don't you ever wonder why?
> Something holds you back, my dear.
> Is it fear?

Meredith scowled. "What do humans know about dragons, anyway?"

"True enough," Carlos admitted. "Now, Meredith, you and I are going to Philadelphia. But, once we are there, I will owe Rupert nothing more, and you shall be free to resume your life as a dragon."

"Carlos," Meredith begged, "You are kind, for a villain. Set me free. I could slink away into the forest and never be seen or heard from again."

"Don't be ridiculous," said Carlos. "You're not the slink-away type."

"You're probably right," agreed Meredith. "But tell me, Carlos, will there be dragons in Philadelphia? And how shall I be free to return to my own land when, as you say, my wings aren't strong?"

"Trust me."

"Why should I—"

She was not able to finish, though. For just then, Carlos whisked his hand over her eyes. All went dark, and she fell into a deep sleep.

"Achoo!" sneezed Carlos. He held a bottle labeled *Here's Lookin' At You, Statue* up to the light. "I don't know why, but even one whiff of this potion always makes me sneeze. Drat, Ferdie, this bottle is almost empty. I won't be able to get any more potion in Deweydaire, since the only place I could find it, Sam's Magic Shop, has permanently closed. Well, maybe this little bit will be enough. *Achoo!*" He spritzed the few remaining drops in the bottle over Meredith and beamed with approval as the potion began to take effect.

When she awoke, Meredith found she could not move. *It had happened.* To all outward appearances she had become a statue. Inside, however, she was still her same dragon self.

When she tried to speak, she found she could not. Her mind, however, was as alert as ever. She soon began to realize that she was going to be very lonely indeed if she did not find a way to communicate with others.

Then she heard Carlos' voice speaking, although she did not see his lips move.

"Hello, Meredith. That's right, it's me, Carlos. Because I made you, you and I can communicate without really speaking. It's called *telepathy*."

"But—are you the only person with whom I can communicate?" Meredith asked (telepathically).

"Yes. Do you have any other questions?"

"Just one. How do I eat?"

Carlos didn't have the heart to answer.

Meredith tried to hold it back, but a single tear trickled down her wooden cheek.

"*Now, how did that happen?*" Carlos wondered. "*Statues can't cry! Or can they?*"

"Ah, but I'm no ordinary statue," said Meredith. *Said!* Even Meredith was surprised at the sound of her own voice.

"Where is that voice coming from!" Carlos demanded, of no one in particular. "Statues can't talk."

He started looking under the table on which he had placed her, in the cupboards, and even in the dresser drawers. He looked everywhere, trying to find the source of that voice.

"Over here, Carlos." Meredith whistled as if she were calling a dog.

As if on cue, Ferdie came bounding in through the open door, with a "You called, master?" expression on his face.

"Sit," Carlos ordered. Ferdie obliged, his tail swishing in anticipation of receiving a treat.

"She was whistling at me, Ferdie. Not you. But what am I saying? This is impossible! Something must've gone wrong with that magic potion I gave you—*you!* Now *I'm* talking to a statue! I knew I should have checked the expiration date on that potion. It must've expired. Yes, that must be it." He began rummaging frantically in his wastebasket for the empty glass bottle. "It's not here. Where could it be?" he wondered aloud.

He looked suspiciously about his hut, but no one else was there, save Meredith and Ferdie who was, at that moment, heartily engrossed in his chew-toy.

"Oh well, I just hope I don't have to explain a talking statue to border officials," Carlos told his dog.

He tied a bandana over Meredith's mouth and stuffed her into his suitcase. He just had a few last details to deal with, and then he would be saying goodbye to Deweydaire forever.

* * *

Now, let us not be too hard on Carlos, for he was a better magician than he thought, even in Meredith's case. Her ability to speak aloud was not due to his failed magic, but because her voice simply refused to be silenced. For, while Carlos had imprisoned her body, he had not conquered her spirit; and he never would. Even in the face of one of the worst possible punishments to be found in Rupert's kingdom, or any kingdom, she had not lost her courage, hope, or dignity. Only that one tear had escaped to roll down her cheek, as her last moment as a living, fire-breathing dragon had passed, and she had become a lovely memento-in-wood of her former self.

* * *

With Meredith safely stowed in the suitcase, Carlos continued with his final preparations.

"Incidentally, Ferdie, there's—uh—something I haven't told you. You're not coming with me on the trip. You're going to stay here with Farmer Klem until I—uh—get back."

Ferdie whined plaintively. He brushed against Carlos's leg and looked up at him with devoted eyes. "Please don't leave me!" he seemed to be saying. Somehow, he knew that Carlos was not planning on coming back for him.

"Sorry, boy," said Carlos, patting him. "Hey, how do you like my hat?" Carlos walked over to the mirror to admire himself in his traveling outfit. Since he had no proper artist's beret, he had selected a green-and-purple-plaid golfer's cap to wear with his silky, swirly, four-colored magician's cape. It had four panels—green, red, blue, and gold—and a glittery gold collar.

"In Philadelphia, I won't have to hide the fact that I'm a magician," he said.

Ferdie whined loudly in protest.

"What's wrong, Ferdie?" asked Carlos. "Don't you think the hat goes with the cape?" He scrutinized his appearance in the mirror. "Maybe not, but 'close enough, good enough,' I always say." Ferdie went back to his braided rag rug and lay down. He put his paws over his eyes.

"I am going to miss you, Ferdie," said Carlos. "Say, I hope that Klem fellow hurries up. I have a train to catch, ha, ha. That's just a figure of speech—or is it?" He scratched his head and said, "That Rupert! He gave me my passport, but he said I'd have to figure out how to leave Deweydaire on my own. That dirty double-crosser! If only I could remember how I got here in the first place! It's funny, but I just can't remember that far back."

Ferdie stuck his soft, wet nose into the palm of Carlos's hand and whimpered plaintively (one might even say, melodically).

"Ferdie, you could have been an opera singer," said Carlos, patting the dog, "but be quiet, please. I've got to think. Now, where did I hear that expression before: 'I have a train to catch'? First, what in the world is a *train*? Maybe I knew it once but forgot." He sat down in his favorite chair, closed his eyes, and strained his brain, trying to remember. Soon he drifted off to sleep.

He dreamed a pleasant dream. He dreamed he was a small boy, eating ice cream with his uncle in a small river-town restaurant, somewhere far from Deweydaire. Up on a ledge near the restaurant ceiling, there was a toy train. It went around and around on a track. Toot! Toot! Went its loud whistle. It woke him. Now, he remembered what a *train* was.

"There's nothing quite like the sound of a train whistle, Ferdie," said Carlos. "It can make you dream of places you're going to and places you're leaving behind. I'm feeling a lot of mixed-up emotions right now, Ferdie."

Ferdie, on his rag rug, was intently engrossed in his chew-toy.

"I once carved a wooden train whistle, out of willow. I wonder what became of it. You haven't seen it around here, have you, Ferdie?"

Ferdie had a guilty look in his eye. This made Carlos take a second look at the dog.

"Ferdie, that's my wooden whistle you're chewing on! Drop it! Oh Ferdie, how could you! I wonder if it still works." Carlos wiped it dry and blew into it. The sound that came out of it was gurgley and water-logged.

Carlos left it for a while to dry out. Later, he tried blowing through it again.

"Well, now, that is an intriguing sound," said Carlos. "I've never heard a sound quite like that, so evocative and plaintive. It makes me think of being homesick and going home. But where *is* my home, if it is not here? Maybe Philadelphia is my *spiritual* home, for I hope to live there as a free man, under just laws, one day. I know Philadelphia is out there somewhere, Ferdie, and I intend to find it."

Ferdie licked his hand.

Now that the whistle had dried out, Carlos picked it up and blew into it.

"Hey, Ferdie, if I cover this new hole you've created with my finger, Ferdie, I can get another note out of this whistle." Carlos played the first three notes (the second two being the same note) of the song many know as "Goin' Home." He could not re member where he had heard it before, but he "must have heard it somewhere."

"I declare, Ferdie, I believe you've improved this whistle." He set it down on the kitchen table and picked up his suitcase, intending to pick up the whistle again and put it inside the suitcase.

That was right before—to Ferdie's great astonishment—Carlos simply vanished—suitcase (containing Meredith) in hand.

It was fortunate for Ferdie that Carlos had left the whistle behind. It was still lying on the table. And Ferdie was a very smart dog.

CHAPTER TWENTY-TWO

"The Great Glass Mountain"

Unfortunately, Peter did not have a "magic whistle" that could somehow whisk himself swiftly across the Deweydaire Mountains. He would have to do everything the hard way.

After traipsing through foothills and sneaking past border guards, he finally reached the foot of Mt. Maurice, the mountain named in the jump-rope rhyme Felix had recited to him:

If Anselm's Way you wish to find,
Seek Mt. Maurice! Don't get left behind!

To Peter, Mt. Maurice looked just as Felix had described it: a formidable, "great glass mountain." Not only was it steep, but it was almost completely covered in sheets of smooth obsidian, a volcanic, glassy kind of rock. Fortunately, there were still areas where there was sparse grass or shrub brush growing, scattered here and there. Still, Peter did not see how he could ever scale such a mountain. If the entrance to Anselm's Way was located on Mt. Maurice, he might as well give up and go home now!

Here was Meredith needing his help, and he was stuck at the foot of a Great Glass Mountain! The obstacles seemed insurmountable. How would he ever find Anselm's Way? He fought back tears of frustration and despair. In desperation, he said a prayer for help to that loving, helping force in the Universe that was recognized even in Deweydaire.

Just then, Peter heard a dog barking. It was the joyful, musical baying of a hunting dog, hot on the trail of its prey. He had heard the sound once and never forgotten it. He turned towards the sound. Just then, a little black-and-white dog came charging up the hill towards him at full speed.

"Here, boy!" Peter held his hand out to the dog. Obligingly, the little dog trotted up to him and licked his hand once in a friendly fashion. Then, with an excited sniff of the air and a swish of his tail, he was back on the trail of—whatever it was he was following. The scent took the little dog back down the slope, the way it had come. Peter watched until he could no longer see him. It was as if the dog had simply vanished—could it be?—right into the side of a mountain?

Peter called down the slope after the little dog: "Here, boy! Here, boy!" He found enough sparse grassy patches that, by stretching his legs to reach them, he could make his way down the slope. Most likely, he was following the very same path the little dog had followed. He kept looking for the furry little creature, but he did not see him. Nor did he see any sign marking Anselm's Way.

The next thing he knew, though, he had fallen into a hole. It was not a deep hole. It was only about four feet deep. It opened into an underground chute, a diagonal downward passageway. It reminded Peter of a tunnel an animal might burrow, only it was bigger than that. It was big enough for a grown-up person or even, perhaps, a medium-sized dragon to easily travel down it.

Peter scooted down the chute for ten or twelve feet until he reached the end of it. Now he was in a spacious underground chamber. He was not hurt, and he had plenty of fresh air to breathe, since the chute opened onto the outside world.

Two cave corridors opened out from that cave chamber. He would need to decide which one to take.

He could not forget Felix's warnings about the dangers of entering a strange cave alone. If he got lost, there would be no one to call for help. He would have to take every possible precaution. If only Felix were here!

On his own, with not enough information, he must decide which of the two cave corridors to take. How he wished he had something with which to mark his path! That would make it easier in case he needed to backtrack. It would also help him find his way back to Deweydaire one day (he hoped).

He remembered how, in a fairy tale he had once heard, Hansel and Gretel, who had gone out picking berries, had made themselves a trail of breadcrumbs so they could find their way home later. Unfortunately, however, the birds had eaten all their breadcrumbs. Well, Peter had no bread to make breadcrumbs, for he had already eaten every crumb of the peanut-butter-and-jelly sandwiches Felix had packed for him.

He rummaged in his backpack to see whether he had anything else he might use to mark his trail. The first thing he pulled out was the headlamp. Now would be a good time to put that on, he decided, before he stepped into one of those two pitch-black cave corridors. He still had to decide which corridor to take.

Next, he pulled out his sweater and put it on. In the bottom of his backpack was that 'super-sized' package of dental floss Felix had packed for him.

At least he wouldn't suffer from cavities. Ha ha. Here he was in a cave, making jokes about cavities. He would have to tell Felix his little joke, one of these days, if—correction, *when*—he ever saw him again. He was going to "think positive."

Suddenly, an idea came to him.

What if he tried to mark his path with dental floss? It seemed like a crazy idea, but … why not try it? It just might work. What did he have to lose?

Without delay, Peter pulled a length of dental floss out of its container. But, to what could he fasten it? He found a rock sticking out from the wall of the cave. It seemed to be wedged tightly into the wall. He wrapped the end of the floss around the sticking-out part of the rock, three times, and fastened the end with a sturdy knot. *There!* That ought to hold it, as long as no animal, person, or dragon came along to disturb it.

He still had to decide which of those two cave corridors to take. As he got closer to them, aided by the bright light of the headlamp, he noticed that, just above the entrance to one of the corridors, someone had faintly scratched some letters in the stone. They were hard to read, but he thought they said, in crooked capital letters: A-N-S-W-A-Y.

Could they be indicating Anselm's Way, the famous cave passageway through the mountains, he wondered? If so, surely things would be easier for him from now on!

He started down the path marked A-N-S-W-A-Y, pulling out floss as he went. With any luck, that one long, continuous strand of floss would still be here to guide him on his return trip (thinking positively).

It was cold inside the corridor, for the warmth of the sun did not reach it. He kept hearing curious rumblings that sounded like they were coming from deep within the mountains. He tried not to worry about them. After all, Felix had told him that Mt. Maurice had not been an active volcano for several centuries.

He tried to be careful not to step into another hole in the ground, now that he knew how easy that was to do. Whether his route would take him underneath Mt. Maurice or around it—underground—he did not know. He would just have to explore it and see where he ended up.

He moved slowly, tentatively, sliding one foot at a time, trying to make sure the ground was solid with each step he took. He could not have been more grateful for that headlamp.

He kept looking for the little black-and-white dog. However, so far, he still had not seen him. As he slowly groped his way down the passageway, he was aided by his determination, his desire to help Meredith, and something very powerful called faith.

He came to a fork in the path where it branched out into a Y-shape. Which way should he go? He decided to go to the right.

After he had gone down that path for a few feet, his boot slipped in something squishy and smelly: dog poop! At least, he assumed it was a dog's, for that was the only animal he had seen. Ordinarily, he would have been disgusted; but now, he felt hopeful. For, if the little black-and-white dog had come this way, maybe Peter *would* run into him again. He hoped so. He decided to stay on this path.

Thus encouraged, he continued down the dark, cold cave corridor, ever grateful for his bright headlamp. After a while, his muscles began to stiffen and ache from the cold. The headlamp put out a little heat, but it was not enough to warm up his whole body.

He thought he would never reach the end of that corridor!

Finally, he thought he could just make out a tiny pinpoint of light, way ahead of him in the distance. As he continued towards it, it grew bigger and bigger, until finally, he arrived at its source. He entered into a big, cavernous "room." Sunlight was streaming into it from an opening in the room's "ceiling" which was, actually, at "ground level." For Peter had been, and in fact still was, underground. Just outside the cave opening, he could see a small "scrub brush" plant barely moving in a slight breeze.

How good the sun's warmth and light felt! He was so grateful, he felt like praying. Eagerly, he ran towards the light.

Then *splat!* The next moment, he found himself face down on the ground with a sharp pain in his shin.

From his new vantage point on the cave floor, he sat up and began rubbing his aching leg. What had tripped him? He looked and soon found his answer. A squarish stone was sticking up out of the ground an inch or so. It looked like it had been put there deliberately. Curiously, the letter E was etched into its surface.

E for what? Peter wondered. Esmerelda? Probably not. *Who could have put it there, and why?* He had to find out!

Using his penknife, he pried the stone free. Underneath it, someone had dug a hole. In that hole lay a stoppered clay jar. Try as he might, he could not pull out the stopper. *What was in that jar?* He had to know!

Without giving any thought as to whether the jar might be a valuable archaeological artifact, he smashed it against a rock. Among the broken shards of pottery lay a rolled-up scroll, frail and yellowed with age. Carefully, Peter unrolled it. The paper was so fragile, he was afraid it would crumble into pieces in his hands. It was not dated. On the paper, someone had handwritten a poem. Fortunately, it was written in his own language. He read aloud:

> To the Reader
>
> Things were fine in Deweydaire,
> Until that fateful day,
> When Anselm's band flew through
> the air
>
> And landed, here to stay.
> Twenty hungry dragons, friend!
> Ponder how you'd feel,
> If you smelt hot breath and wondered
> Whether you'd be their next meal.
>
> But it didn't happen that way,
> I'm very glad to say.

For a small boy in our village
Got them eating oats and hay.

The dragons let us farm for them.
A not-unhappy trade.
Till power went to their heads
And slaves we all were made.

It didn't happen overnight,
But precious rights were lost.
For we were hesitant to fight
And didn't count the cost.

One day they read an edict:
"We own the land, not you."
We bowed our heads and gave in,
Though we knew it wasn't true.

Then Anselm kicked me off my throne
And sent us to this cave—
Thinking we would die alone,
Here in this stony grave.

But Anselm didn't bargain with
A king as smart as me.
For we've found a way to get out
And tonight, we'll all be free.

Anselm won't let the dragons fly.
He tells them if they do, they'll die,
Afraid that if they return home,
St. George's knights will seal their doom.

Godspeed to you—and me, as I flee!

—King El

King El! Peter had never heard of a king named El. Was El short for something else? Peter suspected King El had left in a hurry. Did *E-l* stand for Elvis, Elwin, or Elidor? The kings and queens Peter had known or heard of had all been dragons. He did not think El was a dragon, though. *Could he have been the last human king of Deweydaire? Who or what had been chasing him?*

Peter had so many questions! He realized he might never find out all the answers. The poem did answer some of them, though. For, according to the poem, the dragons had stopped flying because Anselm had forbidden it. Anselm had been afraid the dragons he had led to shelter in Deweydaire would try to return to their ancestral abodes. If they did, he could no longer protect them. Peter thought it was incredible that those dragons had obeyed Anselm, even when it meant they had to give up flying.

As for King El, well, Peter hoped he and his followers had made it to safety. He saw no bones or evidence of carnage to suggest otherwise.

He still did not know why the passageway was called Anselm's Way, but maybe that didn't really matter. Maybe none of this mattered. Or maybe it did. Peter felt certain that at least some of it mattered. Maybe it even mattered a lot. In his history books, Peter had learned that the victors were often celebrated, while the vanquished were forgotten. Peter was beginning to think that King El was too important to simply be forgotten.

He could not take the scroll with him. It was too fragile. It seemed a shame to leave it behind, but what else could he do? He could not wait to tell Meredith about it, though. Surely now she would believe him that—once upon a time, at least—Dewey-daire dragons had taken to the air!

His immediate concern, though, was getting out of that cave. He surveyed the rocky cave walls, searching for protruding rocks he could use as handholds and footholds to help him climb out of it. Most of the rocks he put his weight on seemed sturdy enough to support his whole body. The trouble was: the cave walls were not very close to that opening in the cave ceiling he was trying to reach.

Then he remembered that scrub brush plant just outside the cave opening. What if he braided many strands of dental floss into a strong "rope," lassoed it around that plant, and climbed up the cave wall, holding onto his handmade "rope"? He would also use the rock-ledge footholds as much as he could. After all, he should have plenty of dental floss in that 'super-sized' container that Felix had packed for him.

Basically, he was a pretty strong fellow, thanks to all his years of doing chores on his family's farm. However, he was exhausted from struggling through the cold, dark cave. It took everything he had to "walk up" the cave wall, holding onto his thickly-braided floss "rope."

Unfortunately, while he was climbing up that rope with his body in an angled position, his headlamp fell off. It hit the cave floor with a loud clang. He didn't want to leave it behind, but did he dare go back into the cave to retrieve it? He had barely made it out of the cave the first time. How much longer would his "rope" hold together before it broke?

He still had Felix's glow-in-the-dark stone hanging around his neck. It was pretty bright, as such things went. However, it was not nearly as bright as the headlamp. Who could tell whether he might need that headlamp in the future? He decided he'd better go back for it.

He thought maybe he could hold onto the "rope" with his hands and feet and slide down it into the cave. Lo and behold, it worked! He grabbed his headlamp, stuffed it into his backpack, and prepared to climb out again.

He put his foot on one of the rocky ledges on the cave wall

which had held his weight just minutes ago. Yet, this time, the rock broke off when he put his weight on it. Peter took a tumble. Fortunately, he was not badly hurt.

He wiggled the part of the broken-off rock that was left in the wall. To his surprise, it came loose in his hand. Curiously, there was a little empty space, a niche, left where it had been.

In that space, there was a small, rectangular wooden object, about four inches long. He hated to reach his hand into that space, for fear some creature hiding inside might bite him. But nothing like that happened. He picked up the object. It was a wooden whistle! He blew into it. Nothing happened. He put it in his pocket and forgot about it.

He had no further problems in climbing out of the cave. His rope lasso held tight on the scrub brush.

As happy as he was to finally be out of that cave, all he wanted to do was sleep. He was too exhausted to explore his surroundings right then. Grateful for the warm sun, he stretched out on a large, flat rock. Soon, he was sound asleep.

When he awoke, it was a new day. As a mist began to settle, he realized he was situated on a high cliff, looking down into a pretty valley through which a river meandered, sparkling in the sun.

Before he headed down the mountain to explore its "other side," he thought he would check to make sure his dental floss lasso looped over the sturdy scrub brush which was serving him as a marker was still in place. Alas! It was not! Rocks and rubble had fallen during the night, burying the scrub brush and obscuring the cave opening.

How would he ever find his way back now? Frantically, he dug through the rocks and rubble until, at last, he had unburied the scrub brush plant. He tied his bandana handkerchief to it for good measure.

On this side of the mountain, the obsidian was not one big, magical, glassy sheet, as it had been on the other side. Here, it was broken up into rocks of various sizes: boulders, rocks, and rubble.

Looking down from his high vantage point into the valley below, everything looked tiny, like pictures in a book of fairy tales. He saw a river and a road that ran alongside it, all the way into a town. He wondered if he were still in Deweydaire. He did not know whether just crossing the mountains meant he was no longer in Deweydaire, or whether there was still some additional boundary he would need to cross. He decided the best way to proceed was to climb down the mountain and follow the road into the town.

Oh, yes, he remembered Felix's warning, that "once you leave Deweydaire, you can never return." But then, how could anyone know for sure? Maybe all that old saying meant was that, if you left Deweydaire, you would have adventures that would change you. You would not be quite the same, but you could still go back. The "old you" would not return, but the "new you" would. He was going to think positively so that he wouldn't miss any opportunities that might come his way.

After taking a mental "snapshot" (impressing upon his memory a strong visual image) of the spot where he had exited the cave, he started down the rocky mountainside.

At the foot of the mountain, he found the road and started down it. Before long, he came to a sign, in his own language, that said, "Hamlin Train Depot, 1 mile."

Hamlin. Peter remembered an old story about a town called Hamlin that had hired a "pied piper" to rid it of its rats. After the piper played his pipe and led the rats out of town, the town officials wouldn't pay him. So, he played his pipe and the town's children followed him—all the way into the side of a mountain! They were never seen or heard from again.

Surely, thought Peter, *this* Hamlin could not be *that* Hamlin! He was even more glad to be out of that cave.

Peter felt like he was getting closer to solving the mystery—to him, at least— of what a *train* was. He was curious, too, about those sets of twin metal rails he saw lying on the ground. They were just a few feet apart in width, but they seemed to stretch on and on forever at either end, parallel to the road he was on.

Before long, he spotted a crowd of people standing in front of a long one-story building, waiting for, well, *something*, anyway. Peter wondered what it was. A sign in front of the building said: "Hamlin Train Depot."

The people waiting in front of the depot were all wearing backpacks or carrying suitcases, just as Peter was. From this, he assumed they were travelers like himself. Since they were all looking expectantly towards the left, Peter did the same.

Before long, he heard a far-off whistling sound that seemed to be getting louder. He had never heard a sound like that before. He kept watching. To his amazement, he soon saw a snorting, puffing monster, belching fire and smoke, coming down those twin rails towards him from the left.

So this is what dragons look like outside of Deweydaire! he supposed.

However, as it got closer, he saw, to his disappointment, that it was not a dragon or monster of any kind, but, rather, a machine made of iron. How curious!

Peter approached a man who was smartly dressed in a navy-blue uniform with shiny gold buttons. He had an air of authority about him.

"Excuse me, sir. What is that, please?" Peter pointed to the snorting, steaming monster.

"That's an old steam train," said the official. "What's wrong? You're looking as if you've never seen a train before! Where'd you come from, another world?

"Aw, well, don't worry about it," the official said more kindly, seeing Peter's embarrassed look. "We call that our *Special Express* train. Take it if you wish to have the magical experience of stepping into another place and time. At least, that's what our advertising brochure says."

The official moved on. Peter soon found himself amidst a jostling crowd. He kept his eyes open for a real dragon, but he did not see even one. How was he ever going to find Meredith at this rate?

Then, *slam!* Someone ran into him, knocking both of them to the ground. Peter sprang to his feet, then offered his hand to help up a white-haired old man. He was dressed in a swirling four-colored cape and a plaid golf cap.

"Are you all right?" Peter asked him. "Here, let me help you with your suitcase." Peter reached for the handle. "It sure is heavy! What've you got in here, rocks?" he joked.

"The tools of my trade," the man mumbled, reaching to take his suitcase back from Peter. As he did so, a small piece of paper fluttered from his hand to the ground.

Peter picked it up and looked at it. It said, "One-Way Ticket for the *Special Express* Train." Before he knew it, the man had snatched it out of his hand.

"That is my ticket, thank you," the man said crisply.

"I wasn't going to *take* it," Peter said, embarrassed. "What's a *ticket*, anyway?"

"You don't know what a train ticket is?" asked the man in disbelief. "You have to have a ticket to ride on a train. But this is not just an *ordinary* ticket. It's for a *very special train.*" He cradled the ticket protectively in his hands.

A light was flashing in Peter's brain, telling him to *Follow that man! Follow that man!* Still, the light was yellow, not green.

Of course, Peter's parents had warned him of the risks of

talking to strangers. But, here in this new world, everyone was a stranger—to him. He would never find Meredith if he didn't ask questions and ask others for help. He decided he would have to "trust his gut" (instincts), about whether people were good or bad, safe, or unsafe. He would try to seek out those people whom he had some reason to believe were safe and ask them for help, if necessary.

After all, he had grown up quite a bit, coming through those mountains.

Still, the light was yellow for "caution," not green for "go."

CHAPTER TWENTY-THREE

Guessing Games

Meanwhile, inside the suitcase, Meredith had been startled out of her boredom by the sound of a familiar—if muffled—voice: Peter's! If only she could let him know she was in the suitcase! But what good would that do? Even if he did find her, he could not change her back into her normal dragon self. Only Carlos, or a miracle, could do that. Her situation seemed hopeless.

Maybe she could at least arouse his suspicion, though, so he wouldn't leave the trail. But how? What could she do? She knew she could cry—even if only silently. She had not tried to talk, ever since Carlos had tied that bandana over her mouth.

"Peter!" she tried to call, but no sound would come. It must be the gag, she thought.

Frustrated, she was just about to give up trying to make contact when she noticed that the latch of the suitcase was loose. That must've happened when they hit that big jolt just now, she figured. She had certainly felt that jolt! If only the suitcase would fall open! But even if it did, would Peter recognize her? After all, she had changed somewhat drastically in appearance.

"I was just wondering, sir," she heard Peter say, as he tried to engage the man (whom she knew to be Carlos) in conversation.

"Oh, it's you again," she heard Carlos snap in an irritated voice. "What is it this time?"

"Uh—I was wondering if you knew which train I should take."

Carlos gave an exasperated sigh, as if resigning himself to the boy's presence. "It depends where you want to go. Take me, for instance. I'm headed for Philadelphia. I don't suppose you've ever heard of it."

"No, I haven't," said Peter. "Is it very far from here?"

"It certainly is! It's very far away, indeed."

"Won't you miss your home, going so far away?" asked Peter.

Carlos, his voice choked with emotion, said, "Philadelphia *is* my home—my *spiritual* home, that is. As the song says, it's 'the land of the free and the home of the brave.'"

The irony was not lost on Meredith.

Peter held out his hand to Carlos in a manly fashion and introduced himself.

"I'm Peter Porter," he said, in a voice a little deeper than he was used to.

Carlos did not reach for his hand. Instead, he struck a dramatic pose and said, "I am Carlos the magician. My father was a magician, his father was a magician, and his father was a magician—back to where 'the mind of man runneth not to the contrary.'"

"The mind of—what?" asked Peter.

"That's an old expression my father used to use, and his father before him."

"Okay ... but what does it mean?" asked Peter.

"It means, young man, as far back as anyone could ever remember, or would care to."

"Then why not say so, sir, with all due respect?" said Peter.

"I don't know." Carlos reflected. "I've been using that expression all my life. I first heard it from my father, who heard it from his father—"

"—who heard it from his father, I suppose," said Peter amiably.

Inside the suitcase, Meredith was wishing hard for a miracle.

Just then, from out of nowhere, a little black-and-white dog came running up to them, panting joyfully at the sight of Carlos.

"Ferdie!" Carlos was surprised. "How did you ever find me? You must've followed my scent. Hey, watch out with those paws! You don't have to knock me down."

Thud! Ferdie didn't mean to, but when he put his paws up on Carlos, he knocked him off balance. As Carlos fell, he dropped the suitcase. When it hit the ground, the latch on it sprang open, revealing its contents to all the world.

Peter's eyes opened wide in astonishment. For there, amidst Carlos's polka-dotted boxer shorts, lay a lovely, intricately carved, statue of a dragon.

It was about twelve inches high and a little wider, due to its outstretched wings. Knotty horns sprouted from a high forehead of dark, polished mahogany, curving gracefully into a sleek body. Every line was smooth and elegant. There was not a single flaw (at least, not one worth mentioning).

And yet, the more Peter admired the statue's gleaming wood and vaguely familiar expression of righteous indignation, the more his suspicions grew. Either he could not trust his own eyes or that statue was looking right at him. And why was that handkerchief tied over its mouth? Peter's questioning eyes met Carlos's for one long moment, before the magician looked away guiltily.

"What is going on here?" Peter demanded.

Carlos sat down on a tree stump, his head in his hands. "I'm not a bad person. I'm an artist, a wood sculptor. Oh, I've dabbled in magic once or twice; but I never intended to hurt anyone. Especially not her."

"Hurt who? Peter stared at the statue in horrified disbelief. "You don't mean—"

"—I'm afraid I do," admitted Carlos. "There's a dragon inside that statue named Meredith. Rupert said I could leave Deweydaire if I would use my magic to cast Meredith into a statue and take her with me someplace far, far away—so far away that she would never be able to return. How could I pass up an opportunity to leave Deweydaire? But the moment we get to Philadelphia, I'm going to change her back into her real dragon self."

"Why can't you change her back now?" Peter demanded.

"I've run out of magic potion," Carlos admitted. "But don't worry; once we get to Philadelphia, I'll find more of it, reverse the spell, and set her free. Don't worry. I've got it all under control. Say, you seem like a smart fellow. Why don't you come with us? You might prove useful to—uh—Meredith."

"I don't know," said Peter, uneasily. "I'm already farther away from home than I've ever been. My mother will be needing my help on the farm, as soon as I can get back to her. There'll be crops to plant and goats to tend."

Carlos closed his eyes and struck a dramatic pose, preparing to wax eloquent: "Ah, mothers, *waiting* at the end of the day with supper and a smile! Later, after all the chores are done, there will be stories told and laughter around the hearth ...." His face took on an enraptured expression.

"Uh—Carlos?" Peter spoke sharply to break his reverie.

"Uh—where was I? Oh yes." Carlos clapped a hand intended to be reassuring on Peter's shoulder. "Don't worry about your mother, Peter. She'll manage without you, and you'll be back before you know it. Come with us!"

No, Peter, Meredith tried to warn him silently. *Ask him how long it's been since he's seen his mother.* Although she was overjoyed to see him, she was desperate to protect him. After all, he had come all the way from Deweydaire to rescue her. She knew better than anybody that Carlos would take care of himself first and others later.

"Anyway, I haven't a ticket," said Peter. "I'd have to sneak on board the train and hide."

"A stowaway," said Carlos thoughtfully. "If the trainmen catch you, they'll boot you right off the train. They might even have you arrested. I wouldn't recommend traveling that way, but I certainly can't buy you a ticket. All I have left are these three gold *dracos*, and they're no good here. I had to sell most of my tools, just to get this ticket." He pulled out of his pocket three dracos, embossed with the head of Anselm.

"Any magician who can transform a living, breathing dragon into a statue," Peter said—pointing to Meredith— "is surely able to conjure up one train ticket."

"You don't understand," said Carlos. "It's not at all the same."

"Come on, Carlos, you're just bluffing. Peter needs a ticket!" Meredith tried to communicate silently.

"Meredith, you stay out of this!" snapped Carlos.

Peter stared at him in amazement. He hadn't heard a thing. But if the statue hadn't spoken, then why had Carlos answered?

Now, Peter had always believed in dragons because he had seen them with his own eyes. It was a much harder for him to believe in something he had never seen or heard of before, a talking statue. He took a deep breath and plunged into these strange new waters.

"Meredith, is that really you in there?" He felt silly, talking to a statue.

"Yes, it is, Peter," Meredith exclaimed joyfully. "Welcome to my world—such as it is."

This time he heard her. "Why couldn't you speak to me before?" he asked, suspecting he knew the answer.

"I tried to," Meredith explained, "but you couldn't hear me. I think I had to wait for you to speak to me first, so I would know you were listening."

"That seems to be how it works," Carlos agreed.

"Now, Carlos, how about that ticket for Peter," said Meredith.

Carlos bowed his head and admitted, "I'm sorry, Peter, but I can't just conjure up a ticket for you. I'll not give you any lame excuses. I'm just not as good of a magician as I used to be. My powers seem to be waning."

A train whistle blew. It was the *Special Express*, the old steam train!

"They're boarding," said Carlos. "I guess this is goodbye." He closed his suitcase.

"Don't worry about me, Carlos," Peter cried. "I'll find a way to get on that train."

"Don't do it, Peter! It's too dangerous to ride as a hobo," Meredith cried frantically from inside the suitcase.

However, Peter had not heard her, for he was already running towards the empty freight cars.

Carlos had snapped the suitcase shut on Meredith and was boarding the train—with Ferdie following fast on his heels— when the conductor who was taking tickets stopped him.

"I'm sorry, sir, but that dog can't board this car. He belongs in the baggage car, but you should have thought of that earlier. Just leave him with me, and I'll see that he's waiting for you when you get back. Or, you could take a later train, after you've made all the necessary arrangements for your dog."

"You don't understand!" Carlos was frantic. "I have to take *this* train! It's the only train I can take!"

The conductor looked at Carlos quizzically, wondering what he knew that the conductor didn't about the *Special Express* train. But the conductor was not giving in.

At last, Carlos gave in to the inevitable. He waved his arm in a gesture of helplessness. "Take him if you must. So long, Ferdie."

Ferdie whimpered pitifully.

It was hard, but Carlos's mind was made up. He patted Ferdie's fur one last time and climbed aboard the train.

CHAPTER TWENTY-FOUR

"All Aboard!"

Carlos found a seat on the train next to a window, with Meredith in the suitcase beside him. As the engine started and the train lurched forward, he glanced out, just in time to see two railroad officials holding a struggling Peter firmly and leading him towards the station. Ferdie was right there, too, nipping and barking at the officials' heels.

So, Peter had gotten caught! But what was Ferdie doing, running around like that? Carlos wondered.

"Hey, Carlos," Meredith communicated silently from the depths of the suitcase, "why don't you get me out of this suitcase so I can look out the window. I've already counted all the polka-dots on all your undershorts."

By this time, Carlos had removed the handkerchief gag from Meredith's mouth, at Peter's insistence. It hadn't done any good, anyway.

Carlos blushed. "Smart aleck," he whispered hoarsely, while looking around to see if anyone had heard him talking to a statue. However, as Carlos bent to unfasten the suitcase clasps, he was startled by a tap on the shoulder. It was the train's conductor.

"Sorry to bother you again, sir," he said crisply, "but that suitcase of yours is over eighteen inches tall. According to our rules, any luggage over eighteen inches tall must go in the baggage car. I'd be glad to carry it back for you."

"Just a minute, there's something I need from it, first," said Carlos.

But the conductor, paying no attention, had briskly closed the suitcase, with Meredith inside, and walked off with it, while Carlos stood there stammering, "But—but—you can't." He shrugged helplessly and sank back into his seat.

Meredith resigned herself to the idea of spending the entire train trip in the baggage compartment, surrounded by passengers' suitcases of assorted sizes and their caged pets which she could hear but not see. She thought of poor Ferdie, especially as one of the dogs was just then whimpering rather musically, just like Ferdie used to do.

Just like Ferdie used to do! But it couldn't be he, could it? How could he have gotten on board?

"Ferdie?" she called out tentatively, and, even more tentatively, "Peter?"

Ferdie was indeed loose in the baggage car. He heard Meredith; but he couldn't believe her voice would be coming from a suitcase. He began running about crazily, barking, and sniffing at all the suitcases. Soon all the other dogs began barking, too, in sympathy. What a commotion!

Two porters heard the barking and hurried back to the baggage car, only to find Ferdie running madly back and forth, howling for Meredith. One of them grabbed him by the collar and read the owner's name on his dog tags: Carlos Giordano.

"Giordano!" he mused. "That name rings a bell."

"Isn't he the one who didn't want to check his bag?" said the other porter. "The one in the cape? You'd better go tell him he needs to see to his dog. You're lucky that dog didn't bite you. He shouldn't be running around loose. I'll tie him up."

As if on cue, Ferdie growled, but it was for show only. He was not a mean dog.

The porter backed away and went to find Carlos. He found the magician reclining in his seat with his eyes closed.

"Uh, excuse us, sir. Could you please step back with me to the baggage car? We need you to settle your dog down."

"My dog on board?" Carlos asked. "How could that be?"

Carlos got up reluctantly, stretched, then followed the porter back through eight or nine train cars to the baggage car, as the train lumbered along down the tracks. They had just passed through the dining car when Carlos stopped the porter and said, "Wait a minute, please! I thought I saw someone I knew in there." He quickly peered back through the small round window on the dining car door.

"It *is* Peter!" Carlos muttered aloud. "How'd he manage to get on board? I thought—oh, never mind." The trainmen looked at him quizzically.

Peter was indeed sitting in a dining car booth, squashed like a marshmallow in between two plump, middle-aged, short-haired women who looked like they were twins. The only way he could tell them apart was that one wore a purple suit and had "tortoise shell" glasses, while the other wore a navy-blue suit and had "metal-frame" glasses.

Across from them sat a dignified, thin, silver-haired lady who wore her hair pulled back into a tidy bun. She wore a floral-print silk shirtdress.

Carlos burst into the dining car and rushed up to the booth. He smelled the pleasant scent of lilacs. It reminded him of his mother who had always worn lilac fragrance.

"You poor thing," the silver-haired lady was saying to Peter, "I bet you haven't had a decent meal in weeks, have you, dear?" She patted his hand lightly.

"Well, actually, Mrs. Nestor—"

"When was the last time you slept in a real bed, young man?" Esther Lester (purple suit) asked him, staring sternly at him through her tortoise-shell glasses.

"Well, Miss Lester—"

"You can call me Esther," said Miss Lester, "as long as you say it respectfully."

"Ahem." Carlos coughed and stared meaningfully at Peter.

"Sir, sir," interjected a waiter, addressing Carlos. "Would you like to order?"

"Not now," said Carlos.

By this time three pairs of protective eyes were on him, waiting for him to speak. Peter shot him a warning glance.

"At whom are you staring, sir?' the silver-haired lady politely inquired.

"No one, ma'am," Carlos lied. "I've made a mistake." Then, with a meaningful look at Peter, Carlos continued on to the baggage car to settle down his dog. While he was there, he retrieved Meredith from his suitcase and carried her with him back to his seat.

Meanwhile, Peter was enjoying a huge wedge of chocolate pie, loaded with meringue.

"More pie, Peter?" the silver-haired lady asked.

"Oh, no, thank you, Mrs. Nestor. I haven't finished this piece yet."

"Well, how about some milk, then?" Hester Lester (blue suit) offered.

"Thank you, no, Miss Lester. I only drink goat's milk because I'm allergic to cow's milk."

"You can call me Hester," said Hester, who happened to be a little hard-of hearing. "Well, how about a milkshake then? The sign says they have fifteen different flavors."

"Stop pestering him, Hester," said Esther Lester (purple suit) loudly to her sister. "He said he didn't want anything else." Then she turned to Peter.

"Can you tell us apart yet?"

"No, ma'am, Miss Lester—I mean, Hes—I mean, Esther."

Peter was grateful for their kindness to him, but he was starting to wish for a little time alone. After being in the cave for so long, he was not used to so much social interaction. Also, he was also not used to having such a variety of foods offered to him. Milkshakes had not yet been invented in Deweydaire.

He was not sure whether Esther Lester (purple suit) even liked him, although he did not know why she wouldn't. After all, he had done nothing wrong, except for trying to board the train as a stowaway. He had had a good reason for that, though. If he ever got a chance to explain it to her, he was sure he could make her understand.

Eating that piece of pie had made him a little bit sick to his stomach. It had tasted good, but it wasn't as good as his mom's homemade pies were. Just thinking about her gave him a lump in his throat. How he wished he could talk to her, even just to reassure her that he would be home soon! At least, he hoped he would. He was going to believe that he would.

CHAPTER TWENTY-FIVE

Pestering Mrs. Nestor

It was late in the evening. The silver-haired Agatha Nestor was still sitting in the train's dining car with Esther Lester. Esther's sister Hester Lester had gone back to her seat, but Agatha had not wanted to awaken Peter who had dozed off. In his sleep, his head had fallen against her shoulder.

"So," Esther whispered to Agatha, "what are you going to do with the boy?"

"What do you mean?"

"I mean, now that you've bought him a train ticket, don't you feel responsible for him? Honestly, I don't know why you got involved. He seems like a nice young man, but—what do you really know about him?"

"No more than you do, Es," said Agatha. "You saw what happened. The trainmen had a hold of him. They claimed he'd been trying to sneak on board, but I'm sure he had a good reason. He needed help, so I helped him. That was all."

"Well!" Esther said indignantly. "What about his parents? You can't *keep* him, you know."

"Keep him? Who said anything about keeping him? Although, come to think of it, my husband— may the Lord rest his soul— and I never had any children."

"You can't be serious!" Esther was appalled.

"No, but it's fun to tease you," said Agatha. "Aren't you over-re-acting just a little?"

"Hmpf!" said Esther, still in a disapproving tone. "Maybe so. Just don't forget why the three of us are here: to find that old scroll of Elmer's for the Ancient Archaeological Society. Good night." Esther rose to her feet and headed as primly as she could—considering she was on a moving train—back to her regular seat.

"Good night, Es," Agatha cheerfully waved her on her way.

In another part of the train, Carlos, who had given up on trying to catch Peter alone, was dozing with Meredith in his lap. He had given Ferdie half of his sandwich before settling him down in the baggage compartment for the night.

The next morning, the train pulled into a sleepy town called Hanover to change engineers and refuel. Due to unforeseen circumstances, there would be at least a one-hour delay before the train left the station again. As the train snorted and belched to a stop, Peter looked out the window and saw a "pocket-sized" park next to the station. In that tiny park was a tree which caught Peter's eye; for there was a swing hanging from one of its branches. Agatha Nestor saw it too.

"Mrs. Nestor, I am going to go over to the park and try out that swing."

"Good idea, Peter," Agatha agreed. "We all need to stretch our legs after so much sitting. Keep an eye on the time, though. This will only be a short stop. It's unusual they are letting us get off the train."

Carlos, who had quietly moved to a seat just behind Peter's, had overheard their conversation. He decided he would go get Ferdie and give him a little exercise in the park. With any luck, he thought he might finally have a chance to talk to Peter alone. In his haste, he left the statue of Meredith in his seat.

Peter was swinging when Carlos strolled up to him with Ferdie on a makeshift leash.

"So, what's going on?" asked Carlos, patting Ferdie to calm him down. "Those ladies act like they've adopted you."

"Mrs. Nestor bought me a train ticket. That's all," said Peter.

"You're still with me, aren't you?" said Carlos. "Aren't the two of us good buddies?"

It was awkward, but Peter had to set him straight.

"I'm sorry, but the only one I'm here for is Meredith." Peter's swing was slowing down. He jumped out of it. Then he walked back to the train all by himself.

CHAPTER TWENTY-SIX

A Frantic Search

After Carlos had returned Ferdie to the baggage car and made his way back to his seat, he found, to his dismay, that Meredith was missing. He stared at his empty seat, as if by doing so he could make her magically reappear.

"Excuse me," mumbled a lady in blue cotton work clothes. She was trying to get past him in the aisle. Carlos moved out of the way, hardly noticing her, or any of the others who filed past him on their way back to their seats. His brow was furrowed with worry. He bent down and looked first under his seat, then under the one next to it, but it was all to no avail. He did not find her.

"Looking for something?" inquired a pleasant voice at his shoulder.

"Oh hello." Even before he turned around, Carlos recognized the woman by her lilac scent. It was Agatha Nestor. "Yes, I'm afraid I've lost something of great value."

"What'd you lose, Carlos?" Peter had come up beside her.

"Meredith." Carlos's face was grim.

"Oh, no!" said Peter, horrified. "How in the world—are you sure?"

"She's not where I left her, in my seat."

"You left Meredith in your seat!" exclaimed Peter. "How could you—"

165

"—Calm down; we'll find her," said Carlos nervously.

"What is going on here!" demanded Agatha. "Peter, do you know this gentleman?"

"There isn't time for introductions," cried Carlos. "Just start searching this train from top to bottom."

"For what?" Agatha asked.

"For a small wooden statue of a dragon, about this high," called Peter, measuring off about eighteen inches with his hands. He began walking up and down the aisles in the adjoining train cars, searching all the seats and even the spaces underneath them.

Passengers did not always appreciate a strange boy's requests to search underneath their seats, although he did ask politely. Several of them complained to the conductor. Fortunately, Agatha managed to smooth things over. She even persuaded the conductor to make an announcement in each car for people to keep their eyes open for a missing statue. Unfortunately, no one came forward with any useful information.

The conductor checked his watch. "I'm sorry, but we have to get moving. A train has to stay on schedule," he reminded Peter, Carlos, and Agatha.

"I'm not going on without Meredith," Peter said.

"Now, Peter, be reasonable. She may still be found," said Carlos.

"If she's still on the train," said Peter.

"Peter," urged Carlos, "take my advice and stay on this train with me. Forget Meredith."

Peter clenched his fists in anger. "How can you say that! You got her into this mess; you can't just abandon her now! You-you-you—"

"—Peter, calm down! Why, I've never seen you like this," said Agatha.

"I *said*," said Carlos, "I'd help her once I got to Philadelphia. You know how important that is to me." Avoiding Peter's reproachful stare, he sat back down and buried his face in a newspaper, *The Hanover Times*.

"Thank you for all your help, Mrs. Nestor," said Peter, "but Meredith is the reason I'm here. I have to find her! I don't think she's on the train anymore. I've got to get off the train and keep looking for her."

"Oh, so I'm losing you to a statue, am I?" Agatha Nestor joked. "I don't understand why this statue is so important to you, Peter, but I can see that it is. So, goodbye. I'm glad out paths crossed." She had become fonder of him than she had realized. She wiped away a tear. "Even though I've never had children of my own, I do like them. Why, in the town where I live, all the kids in the neighborhood know they're welcome to play in my big yard. I keep my cookie jar full for them."

She hastily scribbled down her address and gave it to Peter. "Just in case you ever find yourself in my 'neck of the woods.'" She looked like she wanted to kiss or hug him goodbye. Peter was glad she thought better of it, although he did like her. She had been kind to him.

"Will everyone who will be traveling on with us, *please* take your seats," the conductor announced. Peter got off the train.

From the concrete platform outside, Peter could see Carlos; that is, he could see the newspaper covering his face. From another window, Agatha waved at Peter and blew him kisses. He waved back at her as the train pulled out of the station.

Then he walked into the Hanover Depot and sat down in the waiting room on one of its long benches. What in the world should he do now? He had no idea.

Before long, an elderly man in blue-and-white pin-striped railroad overalls and a railroad cap came over to where he was sitting. He smelled pleasantly of pipe tobacco. He was pushing a broom.

"Son," he said to Peter, "raise your feet for me, would you, so I can sweep underneath them."

Peter lifted his feet obligingly.

"Okay, you can put 'em down now. Thanks." The man stopped to study him. "My name's Ben. We'll be closing up here for the night soon. Don't you have someplace to go?"

"Not really," said Peter.

"Well, you can't stay here," said the kind fellow. "It's against regulations. Isn't there someone you could call and ask to come and get you?"

"I'm afraid not," said Peter. "The only one I know that well would be Meredith."

"Meredith, eh. Who's Meredith?"

How could Peter explain to this man that Meredith was a living, fire-breathing dragon who had been trapped inside a statue?

"I'd rather not say," said Peter.

"Okay," said Ben slowly. "So, Meredith can't put you up for the night."

"No," said Peter, smiling.

"I see," said Ben. "Listen, you seem like a nice young fellow. My wife and I run a bed-and-breakfast called Ben and Bertha's. If you want, you can stay with us tonight, free of charge. Tomorrow, we can set about finding your folks."

Peter looked deep into Ben's kind, concerned eyes. His gut told him he could trust this man, but still .... He was trying to be careful.

"I'd be glad to sleep here on this bench," Peter tried once more.

"If it were up to me, that'd be fine," said Ben, "but it would be against station regulations. I would have to report—"

"—Okay," Peter said quickly. "Thank you for the offer."

Soon Peter was following Ben down a stony path to the old man's cottage.

"Here in the country, some of us still live a simple life," explained Ben as he opened the creaky wooden front door. "We have no electricity or running water. It's a little like living in a fairy tale."

Peter thought it all seemed perfectly normal.

"Look, Mama," Ben said to the beaming, round little woman in the flowered apron who greeted them. "I've brought home a guest. This is Peter. Peter, meet my wife, Bertha."

Ben was gesturing with his hands while he talked. Bertha smiled her welcome and began setting another plate on the blue-checked tablecloth for supper. Peter was their only guest that evening.

"Bertha does not hear or speak," explained Ben. "We communicate by sign language, and she reads lips." He continued to sign to her.

Bertha was "listening" via sign language while she prepared their meal of ham and beans, cornbread, collard greens, and sweet potatoes. She smiled and nodded as her husband spoke, translating his words for her with his hands.

Over supper, Peter felt more relaxed with the couple; for they were kind to him, and they seemed genuinely interested in what he had to say. He found himself telling them Meredith's story, after all.

"You mean she was once a real dragon who could breathe fire and fly?" Ben asked, between mouthfuls.

"Except for the flying part, yes; she was very real. Now, though, she is only a statue," Peter said sadly.

Ben pushed his chair back from the table and signed to his wife as he said out loud for Peter's benefit, "That was a good meal." Bertha looked pleased.

Then he lit his pipe, leaned back in his chair, took a thought-ful puff, and said, "Someone took Meredith from—what was his name? Carl?"

"Carlos."

"Carlos—Carlos's seat. It was either someone who is still on the train, or someone who got off at the station. Did anyone else get off when you did?"

"A few people did," said Peter.

"You know, you took a bit of a chance, getting off that train. If Meredith turns up on the train, how will Carlos or Agatha get word to you? Telepathy?" Ben joked.

"Yeah, I know," said Peter. "Maybe it sounds dumb, but I had to follow my hunch."

"I wouldn't call it dumb," said Ben emphatically. "You have to trust your instincts on something like this. We can get you on another train if necessary. Hey, I just thought of something."

"What?" asked Peter, looking up hopefully.

"If the person who took Meredith got off the train when you did, we're probably out of luck. Unless ...."

"Unless what?" asked Peter.

Ben took a last puff on his pipe. "Unless the person who took her was one of the local townspeople. Maybe it was one of those people who service the train when it's stopped at the station. Say, someone who stocks the kitchen or does housekeeping— or should I say *trainkeeping*? Ha! ha! Naw, maybe not. I know most of those people, and they would never take something that didn't belong to them. Just a sec—what is it, Bertha?" She was signing rapidly to her husband.

"You think our neighbor Nelda might have taken the statue? But why? ... You say she just started working as a cleaning per-son on the trains? .... But we've known Nelda for a long time. We've never known her to be a thief. Why would you suspect her, Bertha?"

Bertha signed her response.

"You saw her walk by our house on her way home from work today carrying a big lumpy sack, and she hurried off with an odd expression on her face, as soon as she saw you?" He and Peter looked at one another.

"It's not much to go on," said Ben, "but—"

"—Let's head for Nelda's!" they said together.

CHAPTER TWENTY-SEVEN

A Change of Heart

It was late by the time Peter and Ben arrived at Nelda's stone cottage. Although it was crumbling at its foundation, it was prettily covered with pink climbing roses. Nelda, a thin, nervous woman, came to the door in a faded blue cotton print dress and slippers, her prematurely gray-streaked hair drooping from a bun. All her children were sleeping soundly, Nelda told them, as she motioned them inside. Ben quickly explained that he and Peter were searching for a wooden statue of a dragon. Had she seen one?

"No-o-o." Her hand played nervously with a fallen wisp of her hair.

"Nelda, it's very important," insisted Ben. "This is no ordinary statue. If you should happen to find it, please give it to me at work tomorrow. Good-night, Nelda."

"Good night."

As they were leaving, Peter glanced over his shoulder at the sound of a sleepy child's voice.

"Mommy, who's that?" The little girl was holding a wooden statue upside down by the tail—it was *Meredith!*

"*Sh*, Sandy," her mother said.

Ben's eyes met Nelda's accusingly for a moment before she looked away.

"It wasn't my fault her horn broke off," Nelda said right away. "How was I to know there was going to be a statue in the seat? I was tired and just plopped down without looking."

Until then, Peter hadn't even noticed that the tip of one horn had broken off.

"Now calm down, Nelda," Ben said. "Is that why you took the statue—because you'd broken it? Not that that's any excuse."

"You don't have to lecture me, Ben. I know I shouldn't have taken it. Yes, I was afraid I'd get into trouble if anyone found out I'd broken it. I just got this job. I can't afford to lose it." She gazed fondly at her little girl. "But just look at her playing with it. She has never had such a nice toy. I certainly can't afford to buy her toys on my wages. It's hard enough just to keep food on the table for the four of us."

Peter glanced around Nelda's tidy little cottage, so bare of furniture. His eyes rested on the little girl, Sandy, standing there in her yellow quilted robe, clutching her new-found "dolly" by the tail.

"Cosi, don't let them take you," Sandy pleaded in a worried whisper.

Sandy had spoken to her! That was all Meredith needed.

"Sandy, would you mind setting me down on the floor there, right side up? I'm getting a terrible crick in my neck from your holding me upside down for so long. By the way, my name is Meredith, not Cosi."

Sandy's eyes widened, but she did as Meredith asked. "Mama," she said, tugging on her mother's skirt, "did you hear that?"

"Just a second, honey." In a quiet voice Nelda said, "Ben, go ahead and take the statue if you must, but—couldn't you wait until she goes back to sleep? You see how attached she is to it."

Ben and Peter agreed. However, as it turned out, that was not necessary; for Sandy was now afraid of Meredith and would have nothing more to do with her.

"She *talked* to me, Mama. I mean, she *really* talked to me."

"It's all right, Sandy," said Peter. "Meredith won't hurt you. But you were making her uncomfortable, holding her like that."

"Is she alive?" asked the little girl.

"Yes, inside the statue, she is. A mean dragon named Rupert had her changed her into a statue through the use of magic."

"Oh, come now, you don't expect me to believe *that*," Nelda scoffed.

"Believe it or not, it's true," said Peter. "I've come here to help her get free."

"Now I've heard everything! And just how do you plan to do that?" Nelda demanded, with her hands on her hips.

"I don't know," Peter admitted. "Carlos—he's a magician— might have been able to reverse the spell, but he's on his way to Philadelphia—wherever that is. We'll probably never see him again."

"Hey, come on, folks," said Meredith, "it's not as bad as all that! At least I can talk to people who have imagination, like children— those who believe that nothing is impossible—and they can talk back to me."

Nelda's eyes widened. "I must be going crazy," she said, "but I'm sure I heard that statue talk."

"Me, too," said Ben.

"Please, Meredith!" Peter begged. "Don't settle for so little! You can't move around inside that restricting wooden body. It's too bad Carlos didn't make you with hinges, so you could at least have some freedom of movement."

"You mean like a puppet, to be manipulated by others?" said Meredith. "No, thank you! I much prefer my present situation. It's true I am just an object, a piece of statuary, a toy. To be be- held and admired, even if I am fragile. I have my own private thoughts, though, which no one can disturb. I can speak when

I choose to, or not speak, as I choose. No one expects me to speak, and when I do, it is considered a marvelous thing. More than anything else, I am beautiful, or so I have been told lately."

"By whom?" Peter challenged.

"By Nelda. Isn't that right, Nelda?"

"Of course," said Nelda, surprised to find herself talking to a statue.

"Although, all I really had to do was look in the mirror. Carlos did a fantastic job on me. No longer am I old, battle-scarred, battle-ax Meredith the fighter. While magic may have taken away my power of movement, it has also given me this strange new ability to attract admiring glances. I tell you, being admired is a new experience for me. Carlos has performed a miracle, for which I will be eternally grateful."

"I wouldn't be so sure," Peter muttered under his breath.

"What was that, Peter?" Meredith demanded sharply.

"Nothing, Meredith, nothing at all. I'm just surprised at this sudden change in you. You seem so ... *cold.* You never valued beauty over, well, freedom, and by that, I mean your power and ability to do good in the world. Before, you were much respect- ed as the only dragon who would stand up to King Harold. You organized the Red Dragons to help the human farmers fight off their enemy's yoke, so they could live decent, peaceful, produc- tive lives and not be slaves to the king and his White Dragons. Now, you are powerless, Meredith. Don't you understand?"

Tears of anger and frustration filled Peter's eyes, for he loved Meredith and hated to see her like this. Didn't she care about the Human Cause anymore?

CHAPTER TWENTY-EIGHT

A Monopoly on Truth?

Please, Meredith," Peter begged, "use your voice! Find a way to get out of this shell and become once again the champion of our Cause!" He bent to his knees, imploring her.

Meredith's tone softened as she said, "Peter, I haven't changed—I still care. But what can I do? My hands are tied—figuratively, of course. For once in my life, I am beautiful. Why don't you just go away and let me enjoy what is left to me? Let the Red Dragons fight their own battles. Or you lead them, Peter.

"I certainly can't expect anyone to listen to me, the 'Voice of the Wooden Dragon,' so why should I waste my time trying to get them to? I would be subjecting myself to mass ridicule from the same dragons who once revered me and obeyed my every battle command."

"You're right, Meredith," Nelda chimed in. "Don't listen to Peter. It's too bad about Carlos, but I won't let you down like he did. Why, kid, you're a masterpiece! You belong in a museum where everyone can admire you. Trust me; I'll take care of everything."

"Meredith, please don't pay any attention to her," pleaded Peter. "Do you really want to spend the rest of your life on display, set out on someone's coffee table or being trapped behind the glass doors of a china cabinet?"

"I'll take my chances," said Meredith. "I've got to be realistic."

"Forget 'realistic'!" Peter cried. "You're a dragon, for heaven's sake! You were born royal, with power to use for the good of all. How could you ever be content with what Nelda is offering you? Do you really want to be bought and sold like common merchandise, auctioned off to the highest bidder, or stuck in a museum for the rest of your life? Please, Meredith! Come with Ben and me. Don't let Nelda buy you with her flattery."

"It's whatever Meredith wants," said Nelda, smugly sure that what Meredith wanted would soon make Nelda a rich woman, richer than her wildest dreams. She was sure Meredith must be worth a lot of money to people who appreciated beautiful things and could afford to buy them. And besides, how many statues could talk? She would sell Meredith to the right person and take life easy for a while. It would be the start of a new life for her and her three kids. Why, maybe one day, when they were older, they could even go to college!

First, though, she had to get rid of Ben and Peter before they spoiled all her plans. She walked to the door and made a show of opening it wide.

"Thank you for stopping by, gentlemen," Nelda said with mock graciousness.

"Meredith, please," said Peter. "Don't let this—this—slave trader—sell you like a side of bacon. Come with us! Don't give up. We'll find a way to get you out of that shell!"

Meredith hesitated. "I wish I could, Peter, but I can't—I just can't." Her voice was trembling; for Peter was offering her a lifeline. Was she crazy to refuse it? And yet, she felt she must.

"Meredith," Peter persisted, "may I have a word with you—alone." Nelda grudgingly consented.

Peter took Meredith outside. "Meredith, what is going on? I came here to rescue you, and you won't let me! Don't you want to be rescued?"

"Of course, I do, but it simply isn't possible," said Meredith. "Carlos has gone on without me. By now, he may already be in Philadelphia. At least Nelda has a plan that makes sense."

"But Nelda's plan serves Nelda's interests, not yours," said Peter. "Give me time. I'm sure I can think of a better plan."

"It's too late, "said Meredith, with a touch of bitterness. "I counted on you and Felix. I waited and waited, and you didn't come. I knew Felix was afraid to get involved, but you! I thought you'd come."

Peter felt guilty. He had promised himself that he would go back for her. Then he had gone home, and there had always been so much to do on the farm.

"I'm sorry I didn't come sooner, Meredith, but I'm here now. I came right away—just as soon as Felix told me you were in trouble. Please don't be too hard on him. He took an incredible risk in coming to let me know. He may have once been a coward, but he's not one anymore. Please, won't you come with Ben and me? We won't let you down!"

"At least Nelda has some ideas that make sense in my situation," said Meredith. "All you can talk about is my becoming a real dragon again, and that just isn't possible, Peter—not without Carlos and his magic. Go back to Deweydaire where you belong, Peter—if you still can."

"I belong here just as much as you do," said Peter. "Maybe more so, since at least I'm a human."

"Ah, Peter; but don't you see? The way I best fit into this new world is as a statue. I must accept that. If the best I can look forward to is being admired by people who appreciate lifelike dragon statues, then so be it."

"Meredith, don't give up! Cut this crap out," Peter said bluntly. "You don't have to settle for second best. You know what I think? I think you're afraid to be set free."

Now, no one had ever said anything as rude as "cut the crap" to Princess Meredith before. As offended as she was, she was more shaken by the realization that maybe—just maybe—he was right. Inside her wooden shell, she felt safe—if a bit claustrophobic. After all she'd been through, wasn't she entitled to take life easy for a while? Yes, the statue was confining, but she had gotten used to it. It was her "new normal." She knew firsthand that fighting for freedom meant taking risks. She had taken a stand against tyranny and look where it had gotten her!

But she was not ready to admit any of that to Peter.

"That's ridiculous!" she protested half-heartedly.

"If you were free, you might even learn to fly," Peter persisted.

"What are you talking about? Deweydaire dragons don't fly. That's preposterous."

"They used to," Peter persisted. "I found a scroll buried inside the Deweydaire Mountains that said so."

"Oh, so you believe it, just because an old scroll says so," scoffed Meredith. "I've heard things like that before. They're never true."

"But Meredith," Peter persisted, "didn't you ever wonder why you have wings?"

"Not really. They're attractive. *Were*, I should say."

"But you're still all that you ever were, deep inside. Once you're real again, you'll be able to fly away from here. Don't you see? If dragons could once fly—"

"—Then they could fly again? In theory, I suppose, unless their wings have atrophied from lack of use. But Peter, you can't believe everything you read."

"I don't, but this scroll was signed by King El himself."

"El?" said Meredith, puzzled. "Oh, you must mean that human who called himself 'King Elmer.' You can't believe anything *he* wrote. He wasn't even a dragon. Not to mention, he was Anselm's enemy."

"Oh? I didn't know you dragons had a monopoly on truth!" said Peter hotly. "You were willing to help us humans, but you won't trust *us* to help *you*—is *that* it?"

Ouch! He was no longer talking like the admiring boy she'd known in Rupert's dungeon, but like the man he was becoming who wouldn't put up with nonsense. He was right, but she would not admit it.

"I don't care to discuss it further," she said in a frosty tone. "Please go now."

"Go! Go where?" He gestured helplessly. "Back to Deweydaire? I don't even know if I *can* go back. I had hoped you and I might at least try flying back to Deweydaire together."

"Oh, Peter! You're such a dreamer!" said Meredith. "This conversation is over. I want Nelda!"

"And I'm right here," said Nelda, coming around the corner. She had been eavesdropping from the next room.

Peter realized he had lost the battle. Meredith would not go with him willingly, and he would not force her to go. All the same, Nelda was keeping a tight grip on her. He left reluctantly with Ben, who patted his shoulder sympathetically.

"Don't feel bad, Peter. You did all you could—more than most people would have done."

"I've failed," said Peter. "All is lost."

"Maybe not," said Ben kindly. "What will you do now? Go home?"

"I'm not even sure I can." Peter looked up at Ben. "They say that, once you leave Deweydaire—"

"—Ah, yes, Peter. So they say. But tell me, do you still have your train ticket?"

"Yes."

"Mind if I take a look at it?"

Peter fished the ticket out of his pocket and handed it to Ben who examined it carefully.

"It's for the *Special Express* train, Peter," said Ben. "It's a round trip ticket, and it's good for a few more days. But even if it had expired, I could get you another one."

Peter looked deep into Ben's kind, wise eyes, twinkling blue in his wrinkled face.

"Trust me; you haven't reached the point of no return yet." Ben put his hand on Peter's shoulder reassuringly as they walked back to the cottage.

* * *

That night, Ben and Bertha spread a thick pallet of blankets on the floor to make a bed for Peter (who preferred that to a feather bed) before turning off the lights and heading upstairs to bed. Soon their intermingled snores could be heard throughout the tiny cottage, along with the soft clanging of trains in the distance. It was a comforting, reassuring sound as Peter drifted off to sleep.

His sleep was fitful. He tossed and turned, unable to admit defeat. He dreamed of Meredith, gloriously flying, free forever of her imprisoning shell. Flying, flying, over the sea, with powerful wings spread wide and head held high, the fresh salty air in her face. *Why didn't she want that freedom for herself as much as he wanted it for her?*

In the morning, Peter could eat only a little of the breakfast which Bertha had prepared for him, even though it was delicious, and he had not had bacon and eggs in a long time. He could not help thinking about the meals he and Meredith had shared in Rupert's dungeon. Their friendship had been forged in their shared miseries. It had meant everything to him. He did not want it to be over, even though Meredith had practically come right out and said she didn't trust him to help her, just because he was a human! And after he had come all this way to rescue her!

"Peter?" asked Ben. "'Are you all right?"

"Huh? Oh—yes—thank you. I—guess I'll go now. Thank you for everything." Peter slipped on his backpack, kissed Bertha gratefully on the cheek and held out his hand to Ben.

"Wait. I'll walk over with you to the station," said Ben.

* * *

When they got to the Hanover train station, Peter was surprised to see someone he had longed to see for a long time waiting for him.

"Dad!" cried Peter. He ran into his arms. "How in the world—"

"I took a short-cut," said his dad, with a canny smile. "Let me get a good look at you." He took a step back, still holding onto Peter, and hugged him again.

"Peter," said his dad, "I'm so sorry I wasn't able to get here until now. I know that sounds like a feeble excuse, considering all you've been through. I hope you know that I never would have given your name to Dr. Fitzhugh if I had known that Rupert would seize power and imprison you and Meredith. I'm proud of you, son, for the way you've come through these challenging ordeals."

"Thanks, dad," said Peter. "I understand. I'm glad to see you're not limping anymore." He introduced Ben to his dad.

"Thank you for watching out for Peter," said his dad. The two men shook hands.

"You're very welcome. He's a fine young man," said Ben. "I've got to get to work now; but please, let me know if there's anything I can do for the two of you."

"We will. Thanks again, Ben," said his dad.

"Peter," said his dad, when he and Peter were alone, "are you up for another mission? When Meredith was in the dungeon, Rupert locked Francis the Chancellor in the Tower to keep him from presiding over a trial for her. He's been there ever since. Are you game to help me break into the Tower to set him free?"

"Of course!" cried Peter. "When do we start?"

"Why don't we camp out here overnight and start back for Deweydaire in the morning."

Peter and his dad camped that night in a spot Ben recommended, in the woods at the edge of Hanover. Ben provided them with the necessary tent and other supplies. They fished in the Bright River that ran through the valley. They found it to be abundant with good-eating fish of a species which they had never seen in Deweydaire, with scales that glistened like rainbows. They fried up their fish with hush puppies over an open campfire. It all tasted so good!

After they had eaten, as they were enjoying the warm glow of the campfire's embers, who should come running up but a little black-and-white dog with a swishy tail.

"Ferdie!" cried Peter. "Where'd you come from!" Ferdie trotted up to Peter and licked his face joyfully. Then he sniffed Peter's dad's hand and decided he was "all right." Satisfied, he sat politely, hoping to be invited to supper. Fortunately, there were plenty of leftovers. Peter tossed hush puppies into the air for him. Ferdie took the game seriously and did quite well at snapping them into his mouth.

The next day, Peter, Ferdie, and his dad set out early for the *Special Express* train back to Hamlin. From there, they would travel on to Deweydaire.

Peter was apprehensive about making that passage through the mountains again, but his dad seemed quite confident. He knew a short cut, he said. When Peter brought up what Felix had said, that "once you leave, you can never return," his dad had laughed heartily and said you could never take anything a dragon jester said too seriously.

Still, Peter felt uneasy. In the past, some of his dad's "short cuts" had turned out to be "long cuts." Also, Peter could tell that he had grown, for his pant legs were shorter, and the buttons gaped open on his shirt over his chest. He wasn't sure he would be able to squeeze through some of those narrow cave passages. And if he couldn't do it, how could his father?

What Peter did not know, however, was that, in his pants pocket, his dad was carrying something special indeed: Carlos's "magic" wooden train whistle. With a little help from the imagination, that whistle was good at transporting people—and smart dogs—back and forth from Deweydaire. His dad had found it in Carlos's hut when he had gone there looking for Peter.

Now Peter, too, had a wooden train whistle in his pocket, the one he had found in the cave. He had tried it out in the cave, but nothing magical had happened. That might be because he had not needed its magic before. Or, perhaps, a different kind of magic had been at play for Peter, the "magic" of growing up. Peter didn't have any reason to suspect that the whistle he carried might be magical or have magical propensities, given the right circumstances. Ferdie, on the other hand, had his eye on it. He couldn't wait to find out how it tasted.

Soon, he, his dad, and Ferdie would be on their way to their next adventure. They had done all they could for Meredith, for now. She would have to take her chances with Nelda.

CHAPTER TWENTY-NINE

A Handover in Hanover

The following week, Nelda sold Meredith in an outdoor art auction in Hanover. However, she did not sell her to an art dealer or to a museum, but to an ordinary traveling shoe salesperson named George Jensen. He was an art lover, but he did not have much money to spend on art—or anything else, for that matter. That was especially true on this particular day, for he had not sold any shoes in two weeks.

He had stopped in under the auctioneer's big canvas tent, mostly to get out of the rain. It was the last day of the auction. Nelda had written, in black grease pencil, a cardboard sign advertising Meredith for sale. Over the course of the day, she had marked the price for Meredith down from $50,000 to $5,000 and then from $5,000 down to $500. No one at this auction seemed interested in a statue of a dragon, especially one with a broken horn.

But as soon as George saw Meredith, he knew that he had to have her, even if it meant he had to eat nothing but beans for a month.

"Would you take $50?" George asked Nelda "It's all I have."

"I suppose," said Nelda, handing Meredith over, "if you'll throw a pair of new shoes into the bargain. What do you have in a size eight?"

Meredith was fuming at Nelda's treachery. She had *promised* she would sell Meredith to someone who make sure she was appreciated and admired! Meredith was sorry she had ever trusted Nelda.

George, however, was quite taken with his new statue. He hardly even noticed the broken horn. For him, it only made the statue more interesting. He imagined this was a dragon who had been in a fight or two (little did he know!). He thought it was very clever of the artist to design a statue that looked like it had been crying (little did he know!). He admired the fine workmanship displayed in the carving of the delicate wings. He marveled at its expression of righteous indignation.

However, the next day, when he was packing up to leave his hotel, he found that—try as he might—he could not get his suitcase to close with Meredith inside it. As disappointed as he was, he decided he would send the statue to his sister-in-law, Edith Jensen, as a birthday present. She and her husband, George's brother Knut (pronounced "Newt"), lived in—of all places—Philadelphia! Perhaps, he thought, he would be able to visit them one day and see "his" statue again.

George sent along a birthday card with a note inside that said:

> Dear Edith,
>
> Happy belated birthday!
>
> This gift I am sending you is special. It "speaks" to me. Perhaps it will "speak" to you. I don't want to say more, for fear of "giving away" the secret of what is in the package before you open it.
>
> Say hello to those pipsqueaks Phil and Suse! I will try to get back to see all of you soon.
>
> Love to all,
> George

So, Meredith was going to Philadelphia after all! However, she was hardly traveling in style. The air was so still and close inside the box that she could barely breathe! (or so it seemed to her). It was going to be a long journey. She would travel by air mail, all the way to Philadelphia. Yes, Philadelphia!

Carlos had been right. Philadelphia *was* real.

CHAPTER THIRTY

Meanwhile ...

As it turned out, things had not been going so well for Peter's mother, for she had fallen behind in paying taxes on the Porters' farm. Rupert, who had proclaimed himself ruler over all of Deweydaire, had passed a law requiring any farm owners who could not pay their taxes—which Rupert had raised—to sell their land to the government. Dragons from his new Land Confiscation Division had come to urge Peter's mother to sell her land to them for a fraction of what it was worth. She had hotly refused and, consequently, been arrested.

However, Felix talked him into letting her go, for Rupert had decided to turn the dungeon into a recreational center. He had put in an Olympic-sized swimming pool, as well as a basketball court, pool and ping-pong tables, and a darkroom for his newest hobby, photography. These were all Felix's ideas, but he was letting Rupert take the credit for them.

In fact, there had not been much need of a dungeon anymore, now that Meredith was gone; for the rebels had lost heart and would not fight without her—much to the "Fire Chief's" disappointment. Her leaving had brought an uneasy peace to the land, although certainly not on the terms for which she had hoped.

Actually, Felix had only been joking when he had suggested turning the dungeon into a playroom, but Rupert had jumped on the idea. That left it up to Felix to come up with other ways to deal with the occasional lawbreaker; for Felix was now Rupert's most trusted advisor. He spent more time with Rupert than anyone else because he was the only one willing to play board games with him.

Rupert did not really like being a prince. Oh, he liked the power and prestige that went with the office, but the day-to-day duties of running the kingdom bored him silly. In this regard, he was quite unlike his late father, King Harold, who had put his whole heart and soul into the task of governing Guldavia. As time went on, Rupert became increasingly willing to give Felix a free hand in making royal policy.

And so, Felix found himself spending his days travelling around the countryside, talking to embittered farmers, getting ideas about what had to be done to solve the practical problems of running the country. Over time, he began suggesting reforms to Rupert, perhaps over a game of cards. Here is a typical conversation which Marcus happened to overhear one day.

"Say, Rupert—I mean, Your Highness."

"What now, Felix?"

"Uh—what do you suppose would happen if we cut down on the land tax the farmers pay you?"

"I suppose more farmers could keep their land. I don't think we want to be helping the farmers."

"No? *Oops*, Rupert, it's still my turn. You just went, remember? And what a fine play it was!"

"It was at that, wasn't it!" Rupert beamed. "Now, Felix, what was it you were saying?"

"I was saying that if we cut land taxes, more farmers could keep their land, and the government wouldn't have so much land to take care of."

"Hmm," said Rupert. "I don't know. It sounds like a good idea, but I don't have to do too much looking after the grounds as it is. I have people to do that for me."

"True," Felix agreed, appearing to study his cards, "but think of the paperwork it would save you. Tons of paperwork!"

Rupert's forehead puckered as he reflected. How he did hate stamping that flood of paperwork which crossed his desk on a daily basis! There really was too much paperwork for one dragon, so Felix had suggested he use a signature stamp. The idea had worked beautifully, cutting Rupert's time spent in the office in half. Still, he complained.

"Your turn, Rupert," said Felix. "I think you're going to beat me again!"

"Ha ha! I always win!"

"Yes, you're really good at this game. Say, I was wondering. Have you given any more thought to the tax issue? Shall we go ahead with that tax cut we were planning?"

"Sure, Felix, if you think it's a good idea."

And so it went.

Now, perhaps one might say that it was unfair of Felix to "butter up" Rupert by flattering him and letting him win at games before trying to influence him to make policy changes, but it did make life better for the people living in Deweydaire.

Up to then, Felix's crowning glory had been the new recreation center. Before long, he had convinced Rupert to open it up to all employees of Rhapsody Castle. Since the center would need a manager, Felix had suggested Peter's mother for the job. At first Rupert had adamantly refused to hire her. He had never forgiven her for making him eat oatmeal out of a bathtub. Even if she had intended no insult, Rupert had taken offense.

Eventually, Felix persuaded Rupert to change his mind, explaining that hiring Peter's mother would be a cost-cutting measure because she—as a frugal farm housewife—was such an excellent money manager. Hiring her would save the Palace money. That would give Rupert more money to spend on his favorite pastimes. Rupert liked that idea.

It was a shame she had lost her land, though, and just before Felix's new land-tax cut went through! He wondered if there might still be something he could do, retroactively, to try to help the Porters get their farm back.

However, at the moment, more serious and immediate problems were demanding his attention. The biggest problem was the shortage of food. Due to the failure of the oat and potato crops that year, everyone was going hungry—dragons and humans alike. Even Felix found himself occasionally craving human flesh, just like the uncivilized dragons of old. So far, respect for human life had prevailed among the Deweydaire dragons, but how long would that last? As Felix knew, there were limits to what even a civilized dragon could endure, if hungry enough.

Clearly, something had to be done; but what? Should he look into new farming methods? Require that dragons take farming classes from the humans? As hard as he tried, Felix could not imagine that idea ever taking hold; for no dragon liked to get dirt under his talons—not even Felix.

Well, what, then? Maybe Peter's mother would have some ideas. But Felix hated to ask her, for every time he ran into her (not literally, of course), she always asked him the same two questions: where was Peter? And when was he coming home? And Felix simply did not know what to tell her.

CHAPTER THIRTY-ONE

A Rich Gift

One hot summer afternoon in Philadelphia (Mount Airy to be exact), Edith Jensen, salesman George's sister-in-law, was having coffee with her friend, Joanne Archer, in Edith's kitchen. Suddenly, the doorbell rang. A package had arrived for Edith!

"It's from my brother-in-law, Knut's brother George," said Edith. "I wonder what it could be." With excitement, she cut the tape on the outer box open, pulled out the gift box, and started tearing off the white wrapping paper, red ribbon, and red bow.

As soon as she saw what was inside, though, her bright smile of anticipation faded into a look of disappointment.

"What is it?" asked Joanne, peering into the box.

"It's a statue," said Edith, without enthusiasm.

"Oh, take it out of the box and let me see! May I? Oh, it's exquisite!" said Joanne, holding up the statue and admiring it. "Why, what's wrong, Edith? Don't you like it? Why not?"

"A dragon is not exactly what I'd pick for myself, but it was nice of him to think of me," said Edith. "I prefer realistic art. Also, I've been trying to declutter."

Edith scooted her chair back and got up to get the coffee pot.

"Having a dragon statue around might help you develop your imagination," suggested Joanne.

"Maybe, but I've gotten by without one for this long," Edith joked. "How 'bout another cup?"

"No thanks," said Joanne, glancing at the clock on the wall. "I've got to go home so I'll be there when Joy's bus arrives. We've gotsome special time planned, drawing pictures together."

"That sounds like my Suse," said Edith. "She's always wanting to give me *'magination classes,* as she calls 'em."

"It's never too late to learn from a child, I always say! After all, doesn't the Bible say we must become like little children to enter into the kingdom of heaven?" Joanne picked up her purse to leave.

Edith walked her to the door. "I 'magine you're right," she said politely.

* * *

It was plain to Meredith that this woman did not want her. *The first thing she ought to do,* thought Meredith, *is take me out of this box and put me where people can see me! Would that be too much to ask?*

Meredith had no choice but to lie there, amidst the tissue paper, feeling unwelcome and uncomfortable in her new surroundings.

Just my luck to end up with someone who doesn't appreciate me! she thought glumly.

She tried to peer out over the sides of the box into the adjacent room, the living room. There was not much to see, other than the framed portraits of the family's two children on the wall. The room was decorated all in shades of beige or tan, without any bright colors for contrast. She could not see the carpet, but she bet it was probably beige, too (it was).

She wondered if she would ever be able to feel at home here. Back at Almira Palace where she had grown up, Queen Esmerelda had seen that the walls were hung with rich, colorful tapestries, each one telling a story. She found herself missing her mother, and by "mother," she meant Esmerelda. It surprised her to realize she was thinking of Esmerelda as her *mother*, not as her stepmother.

But why not? Esmerelda was the only mother she really remembered, the one who had raised her, who had missed her so much she'd made herself ill—or so Dr. Fitzhugh had said in his letter. Maybe, just maybe, after all this time she and Esmerelda could be friends again. But what was the point in thinking about that now? Here she was, a statue in a strange land. *Sigh!*

She wondered how long she would have to lie there in that box before anyone even noticed her. She knew of one sure way to get this woman's attention—with her voice. Wouldn't Edith jump if she heard a strange voice telling her that appearances could be deceiving! Meredith tried, but alas! She could not make any sound come whatsoever. She strained and strained until her throat hurt from trying.

Then she realized: how could she expect this woman, who would hardly even look at her, to hear her? Why would she, a self-proclaimed woman of little imagination, ever be willing to believe in the impossible when the possible would do?

And why, Meredith wondered, must she be assured of a willing, open-minded listener before she could utter a sound? Unless she could overcome this handicap, she would be in real trouble. For here in Philadelphia, there would be no one who knew who she really was. It was going to be tough, but she was going to have to convince someone to help her, if she was ever going to win her freedom and return home. There she'd have a voice again, by golly!

There was no time to waste in being angry with Carlos or Rupert, or even Nelda. What was done was done. She did not see how her situation could be any worse, or how it could possibly get any better.

Oh, why hadn't she gone with Peter when he'd come looking for her, when she'd still had a chance, before she'd let vanity and despair blind her to reality, the reality that she no longer had a single friend to stand by her in this strange new world!

She cried herself to sleep.

* * *

The next morning was a Saturday. When the two Jensen children, Phil and Suse, came downstairs for breakfast, they found Meredith still lying on the kitchen counter in her gift box.

"What's this, Mom?" twelve-year-old Phil asked, picking her up out of the box.

"It's something your Uncle George sent me for my birthday," said Edith, their mom. "Put it down; it's not a toy."

"But what's it *for*, Mom?" asked Suse, who would soon be eight.

"For?" Their mom thought for a moment. "As far as I can tell, it's not really *for* anything. "It's not useful like an electric mixer or some other tool. I would say, it is just a decoration, to sit around and look pretty—if you like that sort of thing.

"I'm going upstairs to take a shower now. You kids eat your breakfast in the kitchen."

"But Mom," Phil protested. "Dad always lets us eat in the living room when you're—oops!"

"When I'm not around? If you're going to eat in the living room, be sure and bring your bowls in, rinse them, and leave them in the sink when you're finished," said their mom as she headed up the stairs.

Phil shrugged his shoulders. Suse was looking at the statue.

"It's a conservation piece, you know," she said wisely.

"Conversation piece, you dodo," said Phil. "Don't you know anything?"

"Sure, I do! And I'm not a dodo, either!" Suse retorted. "You're the one—put that down! Mom told you not to play with it." Phil was holding Meredith at arm's length, admiring her.

"She's handmade," he declared.

"Let me hold her," said Suse.

"No, you're too little. You'll drop her," said Phil.

"Give her here. Anyway, how do you know it's a *she*?"

"It *looks* like a she. All right, smarty pants, here. But be careful! You heard what Mom said," said Phil.

Meredith liked all this attention she was getting. She tried to show her happiness, but she had no outlet for any emotion but grief. She had certainly done enough crying lately! She could not see how her tears had stained her face, but Phil noticed.

"Hey, Suse, this is strange," Phil said.

"What! Let me see," demanded Suse, jostling against her brother to get closer.

"Watch out, you almost made me drop her. Look at those tear stains under her eyes."

"Tears don't stain," said Suse, as if she were stating the obvious.

"They do if you're made of wood," retorted Phil.

Suse was studying Meredith, and Meredith in turn was studying Suse with curiosity.

"Phil, she's watching me," Suse said warily.

"That's crazy," her brother scoffed.

"Not any crazier than what you just said."

Just then the phone rang. It was Phil's friend Marty, calling to see if he wanted to come over and play ball. He did.

"Why can't I come?" asked Suse. "I can hit the ball, and I can run fast, too."

"I know, Sis, but this is just for boys this time. Okay? We'll bat a few balls around in the yard tomorrow if you want to."

"Please," Suse begged.

"Bye," said Phil, slamming the front door behind him.

"You'd better ask Mom first!" Suse shouted after him.

She wondered what she would do all day. Her friend Joy was spending the weekend with her grandma. None of the kids on her street could come out and play.

She picked Meredith up out of her gift box and started out the back door. On second thought, she called upstairs, "Mom, can I play with your new statue?"

"I can't hear you. Wait until I come down."

"Okay." She put Meredith back in her box and found other things to do.

She played with her paper dolls for a while. Then she went outside to jump rope. She bounced her ball, looked at some of her favorite picture books, and played "jacks." She practiced trying to snap her fingers. She could almost do it.

She forgot all about Meredith until late in the afternoon when she heard a song playing on the radio about a dragon. She went downstairs and found her mom busy cooking supper.

"Hey, Mom."

Her mom was standing in front of the stove, stirring first one pot, then another. Her face was flushed from the heat.

"What is it, honey? I'm kind of busy right now."

"I just wondered," said Suse. "What are you going to do with that dragon statue Uncle George sent you?"

"Oh, I don't know. I haven't thought about it." Her mom kept stirring. "Why don't you go outside and play now, Suse. I'll call you when it's time to eat."

"Okay, but can I take the statue with me?"

The oven timer went off. Her mom opened the oven door carefully to check on the cake she was baking. "Just be in by suppertime. I'll call you."

Suse might be forgiven for thinking her mother had "tacitly" (not in so many words, we might say) given her permission to take Meredith outside. After all, she hadn't said "no"! The little girl wasted no time in heading out the back door, with Meredith tucked under one arm.

Her mother went to the window, spatula in hand, and called out after her, "Suse! You left your dolls in the treehouse last night! Bring them in when you come!"

Suse turned, smiled, and waved at her mom. She had not heard *every* word her mom had said. She was already too far away at that point. But she had heard one word clearly: *treehouse*. Her mom had given her a good idea: she would take Meredith to her treehouse!

Chapter Thirty-Two

A New Friend

It was not a fancy treehouse. It consisted only of a floor made of boards. It was supported by four posts underneath it ("on stilts," we might say), with rails on the sides. It was securely perched in the fork of two branches of a sprawling oak tree in the Jensens' back yard.

Actually, the tree sat right on the property line between the back yards of the Jensens and their adjoining neighbors, the Baxters. A wire mesh fence between the two yards had cut right into the tree as it had grown, so that the fence looked like it went right "through" the tree.

Now, the Baxters were an older, childless couple who kept to themselves. There were no weeds or bare spots to be seen in their tidy yard. In contrast, the Jensens' back yard looked "played in"—because it was. It had more bare spots than grass, due to the nonstop games the Jensen children and their friends played in it: badminton, crochet, kick-the-can, and ball games of various kinds. There was also a tetherball pole.

As for the treehouse, Phil thought of it as his, but it wasn't *just* his. Their dad had made it clear when he helped Phil build it that Phil was to share it with his sister. This spring, Phil had been too busy playing ball with his friends to use it much, so Suse and her dolls had moved themselves in.

With her short little legs, Suse could barely reach the first rung of the ladder. The other rungs were closer together. It was a good thing she had just grown an inch. At last, she climbed the last rung into the tree house, with Meredith tucked under one arm.

To Meredith, being in the treehouse felt like paradise! Just sitting there, surrounded by a canopy of green leaves and blue sky, was a magical experience.

Suse felt much the same way. What made it even more special for her, though, was playing "tea party" with her dolls. She arranged Matilda, a walking doll almost as big as Suse, Sarah, a baby doll, and Henry, a teddy bear, in a circle with Meredith and herself. Then she remembered the grape-ade she had helped her mom make earlier that day. Wouldn't it be fun to drink it out of her toy cups and saucers! She was sure her mom wouldn't mind if they had some of it. Maybe she could find some cookies, too.

Suse started down the ladder, very carefully. She did not look down. That would have been too scary!

Meredith longed to say, "Be careful!" but she did not want to frighten the little girl, in case it turned out that Suse could hear her. She remembered how Sandy, Nelda's little girl, had been afraid to play with her, after Meredith had spoken to her. When at last Suse reached the bottom, Meredith breathed a sigh of relief.

While Suse was on her way to the kitchen fetching grape-ade and cookies, Meredith felt herself calming down in the warm sunshine. Gentle breezes caused the branches to sway. *This is not bad at all,* she thought. Maybe it was because she was made of wood that she felt so at home, here in the trees. She wondered if that seemed silly. She loved listening to and watching the birds. They seemed to have this "flying thing" down. *What was their secret?*

Meredith looked at the dolls and teddy bear. She felt a little silly that she would soon be part of a "tea party" with them, since they could not speak, as she could. Then—just to test it— she tried to speak. To her dismay, she found she could not! *Of course*, she realized. With no one to listen, she was no better off than a doll or teddy bear! How was she ever going to get home again if no one would listen to her? Besides, she did not even know which way home was.

Like Felix, she had often heard it said that, once you leave Deweydaire, you can never return. But who really knew? Had anyone ever tried? She hated to think of poor Peter, stranded (she assumed) in this strange new world, all on account of her. She wondered if she would ever see him again.

The breeze felt good! She let herself relax and daydream. After a while, she began to wonder if things were really as bad as they seemed.

Suppose, just suppose, she had not really left the realm of the dragons at all— what Suse and her parents might call make-believe. What if it still existed here, in the real world, in the imaginations of Suse and other children like her?

Oh, Meredith knew, not everyone would care to wonder about the daily miracles of life: of birth and death, a bud opening or a butterfly emerging from a cocoon, of a child caring for a kitten or the power of pretending. All she needed was one person who dared to cross over from the world of concrete objects, to take a leap of blind faith into the darkness, like diving backwards for the first time into twelve feet of water, so that she, in turn, could believe that she would be listened to, so that she could speak and be heard. Could she trust this little girl to help her?

Just then. Suse came back with her pockets full of "store-bought" chocolate chip cookies and a pitcher of grape-ade— what was left of it—in one hand (she had spilled a little coming back up the ladder).

"Now we can have a party," Suse said gaily to her guests. "Here you are, Matilda, Sarah, Henry, and—oh, I forgot to ask your name."

Meredith gulped hard and took the plunge. "It's Meredith."

Suse looked a little startled at hearing Meredith's voice. "I knew there was something special about you! I could see it in your eyes. So, you can talk, huh."

"Yes, but only, it seems, if people are listening," said Meredith. "I'm glad I didn't scare you. Do you like to be called *Suse*?"

"Yes. It's short for Susie."

"Okay, Suse," said Meredith. "You see, I had to take a chance, because I'm a prisoner inside this statue and a stranger here in this land. I need you to help me get back home."

"Of course, I'll help you!" said Suse.

"That's great," said Meredith. "Maybe you'll be able to think of some ideas we can try. I made a big mistake in not letting Peter rescue me before."

"Peter? Who's that?" asked Suse.

"Peter was—is still, I hope—my good friend. We were in the dungeon together in Rupert's kingdom, in a far-off land called Deweydaire."

"Who's Rupert?"

"He's my cousin, a silly dragon who happened to be born the son of a king. He took the throne when my uncle, King Harold, died. Since then, he has made a travesty, a farcical circus, out of justice in the land."

"But why would he do a thing like that?" Suse asked, pouring grape-ade—seconds—into five tiny cups.

"Because he only cared for the power of ruling, not for the privilege of serving the people," Meredith explained.

Suse nodded wisely. "So, he put you in jail?"

"Yes, the dungeon at Rhapsody Castle," said Meredith. "Rupert had a magician cast me into this statue as a punishment for speaking out against injustice and fighting for the rights of humans who were being oppressed by the dragons."

"How awful!" exclaimed Suse.

"Yes," Meredith continued. "He wanted to keep me from encouraging others to do the same. Selfish, greedy dragons who had all the money and power were passing unfair laws that made it hard for poor folk to raise enough food to feed their families."

"Do you mean farmers?" asked Suse, catching on quickly.

"Yes," said Meredith. "They were being heavily taxed by King Harold. I helped them to organize, so that, by speaking together, with one voice, they would be heard."

Meredith suddenly had a flash of insight. How could she have forgotten such an important lesson? Maybe she couldn't do this alone, but with the help of others, who knew what might be possible?

Suse interrupted her thoughts.

"I have a question. Is Meredith a girl's name or a boy's name?"

"It could be anyone's," Meredith replied, "but I am female."

"I thought so. I told my brother—"

"—Suse!" Her mom called loudly from the house.

"I'm in the treehouse, Mom!"

"It's time to eat!"

"Coming!" Suse started carefully down the ladder. "I'll be back tonight if I can," she told Meredith.

"Well, don't come if it's dark out. You might fall, trying to climb that ladder in the dark."

"I'll be careful. Don't worry," said Suse as she stepped onto the ground. She ran back to the house and went inside.

"Suse, would you please set the table," said her mom. "And don't forget, it's your turn to dry the dishes tonight."

"Aw, Mom, couldn't Phil do it tonight?" Phil and their mom exchanged glances.

"I've already cut the grass and taken out the trash today," said Phil. "Come on, Suse, don't try to get out of it. It's your turn."

"I could cut the grass next time," Suse offered.

"When you get a little older, we'll let you. Looks like you're drying dishes tonight, Suse." Her mom handed her a stack of plates.

"Mabel, Mabel, set the table, just as soon as you are able," Phil teased Suse, reciting lines from one of her jump-rope rhymes.

* * *

Suse could hardly wait for the family to finish its evening meal, even though they were having some of her favorite foods: fried chicken, corn-on-the-cob, and chocolate cake. Then there were the dishes to tend to. Finally, she was free to go back out to the treehouse! Or so she thought ....

Her parents were settled in the living room. Her mom was un-tangling some yarn the family's black cat, Bozo, had gotten into. Suse's hand was on the doorknob. She was so close. She was just about to make her escape into the back yard, when her mother stopped her:

"Where're you going, Susie?"

"Oh, just out."

"Honey, I don't think that's a good idea," said her mom. "Hear the wind? There's a real storm brewing out there. And besides—" she glanced at the clock— "Yes, just as I thought. It's bedtime. Why don't you go and brush your teeth, and I'll come up and tuck you in, just as soon as I finish untangling this yarn. Bozo got into my knitting basket again." Bozo, the family's black cat, looked up with mild interest, then went back to grooming him-self complacently.

Suse started to protest. However, seeing her mom's firm ex-pression, she changed her mind and started slowly toward the stairs—even though she was not one bit sleepy.

"Don't forget my kiss, Susie-Q," said her dad from his recliner, lifting his eyes from his book. "G'night, now." He switched on the wooden radio which sat on the table next to his reclining chair.

Suse started up the stairs slowly. Just as she reached the top step, a song on her dad's radio caught her ear. She thought it was beautiful, although she couldn't make out many of the words. Two words she did make out were "Norwegian wood." Quietly, she sat down on the top step—just for a little bit—to listen to it.

"Knut," she heard her mother say, drowning out the song, "What is this book you've been reading? Let me see. Oh, it says on the book jacket it's a biography of Christian Jensen Lofthus. Hmm. It says he was an important figure in the history of Norway."

"Yes, dear. Please don't lose my bookmark. I'll be giving a talk about him at the local library next week. It's part of a series on books about saints, martyrs, and other heroes who have aided the human struggle for human freedom and dignity."

"How interesting! I'll be sure to attend." Suse's mom began to read aloud from the book's "Summary":

Christian Jensen Lofthus was a Norwegian hero. In 1786–87, a time when Norway was ruled by Denmark, he went before the Danish Crown Prince Frederik and spoke out on behalf of Norwegian farmers who were being treated unjustly by the Danes. The mission had seemed successful. Lofthus thought he had convinced the King that change was necessary, so he had returned home. Not long afterwards, though, the King's men came to his home and arrested him, saying he had incited the Norwegian farmers to riot. He was thrown into prison where he spent the rest of his life. In the year after he died, he was awarded a full pardon, posthumously.

"That poor man!" said Suse's mom. "How did you come to be interested in him, anyway? Was it because his middle name is the same as our last name?"

"Sort of," admitted her dad. "I was looking in the encyclopedia for an article on *The Jetsons*. that old cartoon television show. As I was turning the pages, his name caught my eye. I found myself wanting to know more about him."

"Oops! There goes your bookmark! Sorry. Hey, look at this! Your bookmark is an advertisement for a magician!"

Suse, still sitting on the top step, had been starting to get sleepy. She had been just about to tiptoe off to bed when she heard the word *magician*.

Suse's mom began to read the blue paper "flyer" out loud:

> Do you need a magician for your next children's party? The Great Jordano is now available. Call 555-555-5555. Also ask me about my custom-made wooden clocks and lifelike statues.

Magician! Statues!

"Knut, didn't I tell you?" said her mom. "I've been looking for a magician for Suse's birthday party next month."

""Yes, but—well, he's not your ordinary magician, Edith. He rides the same bus I do in the mornings. He'd be hard to miss in a crowd, for he always wears the same colorful cape and plaid golf cap. He says he just got out of Elmira—only he says it kind of funny, like *Almira*. He doesn't seem to want to talk about it, though."

"Maybe he's an escape artist, like Houdini," suggested her mom.

"There's another thing," said her dad. "He seems obsessed with finding a statue of a dragon about eighteen inches tall. He says he needs it for his new magic act."

A statue of a dragon! Oh no! Suse, still crouched on the stairs, clapped her hand over her mouth to keep from crying out.

"Knut, your brother just sent me a statue like that for my birthday. Isn't that a weird coincidence! I wasn't sure if I was going to keep it, though, since I've been trying to declutter the house. I thought I might donate it to charity. Is there anything *you'd* like to donate? How about those golf clubs of yours, up in the attic?"

"Uh—Edith, I've got a great idea," he said, changing the subject. "Instead of donating the statue to charity, why don't we see if old Jordano wants it?"

"I guess we could," said her mom, thoughtfully. "I hadn't decided for sure to get rid of it, though. What if your brother comes to visit? His feelings might be hurt if he doesn't see it here."

"Yeah, that could be awkward," her dad agreed. "It's up to you. I just thought maybe we could help out a struggling newcomer to our country."

"Well, why don't you give him a call. Maybe we can hire him for Suse's birthday party."

"Okay" said her dad. "It's too late to call him tonight, but I will look for him at the bus stop tomorrow morning. He's always there at six a.m. sharp, even on the weekends. If he's interested, I'll bring him over to the house and we can give him the statue first thing in the morning."

First thing in the morning! Oh no! Suse sprang to her feet quickly, forgetting how the old wooden stairs would creak.

"Suse, are you in bed?" Her dad sounded like he was in no mood for "funny business."

In two lickety-split seconds she could truthfully answer, "Yes," although thunder crackled in protest. She pulled the covers up over her head.

First thing tomorrow! Somehow, Suse had to keep Meredith from falling into the clutches of this magician, Jordano. *But how?* Maybe an idea would come to her in her sleep.

CHAPTER THIRTY-THREE

A Familiar Game

Suse awoke to the chirping of birds. It was still dark out. She stumbled down the hallway to Phil's room to borrow his flashlight. He would not mind. He usually kept it in his dresser, next to his bed. *Thud!* Her foot collided with his football helmet. *Ouch!*

"Huh?" Phil stirred at the noise.

"Can I borrow your flashlight?" she whispered.

"Top drawer," he muttered, and went back to sleep.

Minutes later, Meredith spotted Suse's bobbing light making its way across the lawn to her.

"'Morning, Suse," Meredith greeted her as the little girl's face appeared at the edge of the treehouse. "Isn't it a glorious one? I haven't slept so well in ages! I could stay in this treehouse forever." Suse hoisted herself up from the top rung into the treehouse.

"I wish you could, too, Meredith, but you can't. We've got to find a way to set you free today." Suse plopped down cross-legged beside her on the treehouse floor.

"Today! What's the hurry?" asked Meredith. "You and I were just getting to know each other. I was hoping we could have at least one more tea party first."

A faint flash of lightning lit up the sky, followed by a rumble of distant thunder. A storm might break at any minute, or it might pass over them. Suse vaguely remembered her mom telling her not to be in the treehouse if there was a storm brewing.

"I wish we could have another tea party, too, Meredith, but we can't. I don't want to worry you, so I won't go into details; but we have to set you free today. This may be the only chance I have to help you. Did you think of any ideas that we could try?"

"No," Meredith had to admit. "How about you?"

"I had a dream about you last night," said Suse. "You were flying, flying home, across the sea. Do you live across the sea?"

"I think so .... I really don't know. I was in a suitcase and couldn't see anything. But it doesn't matter because I can't fly."

"You mean, you don't believe you can," said Suse bluntly.

"I *can't*," said Meredith. "I've never been able to fly, so why would I be able to now?"

"All I know is, I dreamed you could fly, and you were flying home."

"But my wings don't work, I'm sure," protested Meredith. "Even when I was in my dragon body—"

"—You mean you used to be a *real dragon*?" Suse stared at Meredith in amazement.

"Sure! I thought you knew that."

"Well, if you used to be a real dragon, then you still are one, inside," said Suse, with the practical wisdom of an almost-eight-year-old. "That means you can fly, whether you believe you can or not."

"But I *can't*!" Meredith protested. "I can't get out of this wooden shell without Carlos."

"Carlos—who's he?"

"He's the magician who cast me into this statue. He promised to change me back into my real dragon self once we got to Philadelphia, but he went on without me. I'll never find him now," said Meredith in despair.

The skies were darkening, threatening an imminent downpour. Would the rain hold off?

Suse was starting to put two-and-two together.

"Meredith, does Carlos ever use another name?"

"What do you mean? Wait a minute …. I think his last name is Giordano."

Giordano! That was the name on the flyer her mom had read!

"Do you trust him, Meredith?" Suse asked.

"Not more than absolutely necessary."

"Do you trust me?"

"Well, you're an eight-year-old child, but, yes, I guess so," said Meredith. "I know you want to help me."

"That's good. Let me think about this." Suse was quiet, sitting cross-legged, her elbows on her knees and her head in her hands.

Finally, she said, "Meredith, you don't need Carlos. All you need is to believe in yourself and free up your 'magination."

"Suse, I know you mean well, but it's just not that simple."

Suse wasn't listening. She was lost in thought, cooking up her scheme.

She snapped her fingers. "I've got it!" she cried. "We'll play a game I know called Statues. It's lots of fun. Since you're already a statue, we'll make up our own version. We'll play it in reverse."

"Suse," began Meredith gently. "I just don't see how just playing a game—even statues in reverse—could unleash the power to set me free."

"It has to do with the 'magination," Suse explained confidently. "Let me tell you how you play the game. We might have to change some of the rules, though. Usually, you have a bunch of kids and play it on the grass. One kid gets to be the shopkeeper, and another gets to be the buyer. The shopkeeper swings all the kids by their arms, 'round and 'round. Then he lets go, gently, and they fall onto the grass. Each kid has to stay the way he lands—frozen, like a statue.

"I made up a little rhyme for the shopkeeper to say as he swings each kid. Would you like to hear it?"

"Okay," said Meredith half-heartedly.

Suse chanted her verse:

Statue, Statue, round and round,
Freeze when your feet touch the ground.

"That's lovely, Suse, but—"

"—Next, the buyer comes along," continued Suse confidently. "As he touches each kid—each statue—his touch brings each one back to life. When that happens, each kid makes crazy movements, trying to get the buyer's attention. The buyer chooses his favorite, and that kid becomes the next shopkeeper. Then the game starts over."

"I'm sure it's fun, Suse," said Meredith gently, "but I just don't see how it could work. I'm already a statue, and we don't have a bunch of kids. Plus, we're not on the grass. We're in a treehouse."

Suse was undeterred. "Like I said, we're making up our own version. It's the 'treehouse, reverse, two-person' version. Here's what we'll do. I'll swing you 'round and 'round and say the magic words. Then, when I let go, you'll be free!" She was supremely confident her plan would work.

"First, though," Suse went on, "we've got to move Sarah, Matilda, and Henry out of the way. Sorry, guys. It's just for a little while." She wrapped the three of them up in a doll blanket and dropped them as gently as she could onto the grass below.

Then she picked Meredith up.

"Wait, Suse, please!" said Meredith. "I'd hate for your idea to fail. Then we'd both be disappointed."

"It'll work. But if it doesn't, we'll just try something else. What's holding you back, anyway, Meredith? Is it fear?"

Carlos had asked her that same question once. "I don't really know," she said.

"Well, then, believe this will work and it will," said Suse. "I believe it will work, and I believe in you."

Believe. Wasn't that what Peter had been trying to tell her all along? Oh, if only she could believe again, that she could do something that would make things change for the better, that there was hope for her future, that she could be free again!

"Let's go for it!" said Suse. As she got ready to twirl about, Meredith felt gripped by sheer terror.

"Wait, Suse! I'm almost ready. Just give me a second."

Here comes the end! she was thinking. *I'll be shattered into a million tiny pieces, all over the yard, and I'll—*she stopped herself. Wasn't that exactly what she had been longing for, to be free of that confining wooden body, which kept her from being her true self, an honest-to-goodness, fire-breathing dragon who cared more about going home where she belonged and setting her country to rights than she did about being admired for her looks and not her deeds?

If being broken on the ground was the worst thing she had to fear, then what was there to fear? There was only one way she could fail, and that was not to even try. Even if she had suffered disappointments and failures in the past, she had to try one more time.

"Ready?"

"Blast off!" cried Meredith—before she could lose her nerve.

Suse held onto her tightly and twirled with her 'round and 'round. They grew dizzier and dizzier until it seemed like anything could happen.

Breathlessly, Suse chanted her verse-in-reverse:

Statue, statue, round and round
Don't let your feet touch the ground!

Suddenly, an ear-splitting crack of thunder startled Suse. Her neat circular swing turned into a crazy elliptical orbit. She accidentally whacked Meredith hard into the tree trunk. The rain had made her hands wet and Meredith slippery. She didn't mean to, but she accidentally let go of her.

Oh no!

Suse buried her face against the tree trunk as the sky-splitting thunder seemed to engulf them both. When she dared to look, the statue she had known as "Meredith" lay broken on the ground.

"Meredith," Suse whispered, choking back sobs.

"Up here, Suse!" Meredith cried out.

And what Suse saw next was a sight she would never forget, for there above her was a life-sized dragon—*the real Meredith!*

She was a thing of glorious color, her scarlet body covered with glistening reddish-gold scales, her wings shimmering like metallic rainbows, just like a phoenix against the rosy dawn. Only the faintest trace of those old, ugly battle scars remained.

Meredith hovered in the sky, then spread powerful—yes, powerful, for they were new—wings, and *whoosh!* She swept away into the morning sunrise.

Suse waved and called out, "I told you it would work!" as Meredith circled the tree house at high speed.

"I do seem to be flying, don't I?" She did a few more turns about in the sky, making loop-de-loops, just for fun. She felt one with the weather. Exhilarated, she danced joyfully in the rain. Suse looked on from the treehouse, equally drenched and happy.

They both knew she had to go.

"Goodbye, my friend, and many thanks!" Meredith said fervently. "I couldn't have done it without your help. Or Yours," she added, looking up to the heavens.

Suse stood in the treehouse watching and waving until all that was left was a faint dragon tracing in the billowy clouds.

"Suse!" Her mom was standing at the base of the tree, holding an umbrella. "C'mon down, you're getting wet. Breakfast is ready."

Suse climbed carefully down the slippery ladder rungs, holding onto the rails.

"Mom, did you see? The dragon, in the clouds?" Hopefully, she looked into her mother's eyes.

"You know," her mom mused in wonder, as she slipped a rain poncho over Suse's head, "I think I did!" Then she spotted the pieces of broken statue scattered about on the ground. "Oh Suse! What a mess, and all over the Baxters' yard!" But she was smiling like a co-conspirator.

"Come on, Mom," said Suse, taking her mother's hand eagerly. "Let's go inside and draw some pictures together." Giggling and holding hands, they took giant steps through the wet grass back to the house. There, on the back deck, stood her father and a stooped, white-haired old man in a colorful cape, gazing up into the sky together in awe.

Meredith flew mightily, enjoying the sensation. At first uncertain of her bearings, she trusted her dragon instincts to carry her home. It would take her days, even at 180 miles per hour, which is about what she was clocked at by several U.S. Air Force intelligence officers over Omaha, Nebraska who suspected her of being an unidentified flying object ("UFO").

CHAPTER THIRTY-FOUR

"Sure, You're Meredith!"

Meredith flew into Almira the following week. Exhausted, she stretched out in a deserted field and slept. When she awoke, she found herself surrounded by curious onlookers, both dragons and humans. Someone had covered her with a blanket.

"May we help you?" asked a fellow dragon.

Always a princess, Meredith rose to her feet, holding her blanket around her. "I am Meredith," she said. "Take me to the queen."

There were murmurs of disbelief from the dragons in the crowd, while the humans watched in silence.

One dragon jeered, "Hey, wasn't there someone here yesterday claiming to be Meredith? And the day before that, and the day before that?"

Another leered in her face. "If you're Meredith, where've you been all this time? The queen is ill, or didn't you even know or care?"

"The *real* Meredith would have come home a long time ago to set matters to rights. The *real* Meredith is probably dead by now," said another.

A pompous, heavy-set dragon in a business suit stepped forward, his gold watch dangling from his vest pocket, and cleared his throat. "The real Meredith couldn't fly. Not to mention, she was battle-scarred, but you—well, you're very beautiful." He took a step back, blushing.

But Meredith was unconcerned with compliments just now. She held her hands out in entreaty. "Won't anybody believe me and send for the queen? Why would I pretend to be Meredith if I'm not?"

"That's obvious," one dragon smirked. "Meredith will inherit the throne."

"Where's your identification card?" one official-looking dragon demanded. "Don't you have anything with your name on it?"

Meredith shook her head. "I've been far, far away from here, a prisoner in a strange land. I came home as soon as I could. I'm very tired; it's been a long trip." Exhausted and overwhelmed at not being recognized in her own country, she fainted dead away.

At that moment, Dr. George Fitzhugh came running up. *Could it be Meredith, at last? Yes, it must be!* Although she had changed somewhat in appearance, he recognized her by the ring on her finger. It was the green peridot ring her grandfather had given her.

"Someone, run to my office and fetch some smelling salts," he cried.

However, before they could arrive, Meredith had raised her head groggily.

"Welcome home, Princess Meredith." Dr. Fitzhugh gave a solemn bow. "May I take you to the queen?"

CHAPTER THIRTY-FIVE

A Family Reunion

When Meredith first gazed upon her stepmother Queen Esmerelda, lying in bed, so pale and frail, she realized that all her old hard, bitter feelings towards the queen had melted away a long time ago. Taking Esmerelda's cold scaly dragon hand in her own, Meredith brushed her stepmother's cheek with a kiss. Dr. Fitzhugh hoped for a miracle.

"I'll leave the two of you alone," he said, bowing and taking his exit.

Meredith sat at Esmerelda's bedside and talked to her, even though the queen was still in her fairy-tale sleep state and probably could not hear her (unless Meredith's touch and kiss had already performed its magic, and Esmerelda was now just pretending).

Meredith told Esmerelda how much she loved her and how sorry she was that she had been away for so long. Once or twice, she thought she had seen Esmerelda's eyes blink. When she told the queen about some of that silly jester Felix's antics, she thought she saw Esmerelda's mouth turn up—just a little—in a smile. But when Meredith got to the part about how Rupert had had her turned into a statue, that was when the feisty queen opened her eyes.

"Where's that Rupert! Just wait till I—"

"Mom!" cried Meredith! "Welcome back!"

"Welcome back yourself," retorted the queen. "Come closer so I can get a good look at you, my daughter! We have so much to talk about. I've missed you—so much! I'm sorry I behaved badly and made you think I wanted you to leave. Will you ever forgive me?"

"I already have, Mom!" said Meredith. "I'm sorry I hurt you, too."

"Apology accepted. You must be tired. Why don't you rest, and we can talk more tomorrow," suggested Queen Esmerelda. "I can't wait to tell you about my dream. I dreamed you were *flying*, of all things!"

"Mom, I *was* flying!" said Meredith. "I flew home to Deweydaire."

"Oh my! You left Deweydaire and came back again!" said Queen Esmerelda. "I didn't think such a thing was possible. Say, do you think you could teach me how to fly? Flying would be an excellent skill for any dragon to have! Why, maybe you and I could start a school to teach all the little dragons to fly. Tell me, how did it feel to be flying?"

"It was wonderful, Mom," said Meredith, laughing. "I can't even describe it."

"I bet," said the queen. "After you've rested up a little, maybe we can bake some cookies together. And then we can play that board game you always used to beat me at. You were always good at games. But that can wait.

"There's just one thing more I want to do today," the queen continued. "Give me your hand." She slipped off her signet ring—the ring only a queen could wear—and put it on Meredith's finger. It fit perfectly.

"Mom, does this mean—"

"—Yes," said Esmerelda, "I retire. It's your turn to be queen now—provided you'll teach me how to fly, and soon! Okay, now go get some rest, Meredith. I'll see you tomorrow. Fitzhugh, that goes for you too. Everybody out of here! This is enough excitement for one day." Soon she was fast asleep normally, snoring loudly, with a happy smile on her face.

"You know," remarked Dr. Fitzhugh, "if you get someone to turn that E sideways, you'll have an M. Just a suggestion, Your Majesty." He made a half-bow to Meredith.

"Hmm. Fitzhugh, I hardly even expected to return home, let alone become queen. Do me a favor, will you? Say nothing to anyone about this until I've had a chance to think it over? I want to do what's best for Almira."

"Are you sure? I mean—if some of us were offered the job of running the country—"

"Fitzhugh, are you the 'dragon who would be king'?" Meredith teased him.

At that moment, Dr. Samson burst into the room.

"I've found it!" he cried, waving a book.

"Found what?" asked Dr. Fitzhugh and Meredith together.

"The book that tells how to awaken the queen!" The doctor held up *Hypnosis for Beginners.* "It's right here, in chapter thirty-five."

"Fred—" began Dr. Fitzhugh gently.

But Dr. Samson could wait no longer. "Now, Your Majesty, when I snap my fingers, you will wake up." Dr. Samson eagerly snapped his fingers loudly near the Queen's ear.

The Queen woke with a start. "What's going on?" she asked.

"It worked!" cried Dr. Samson, jumping into the air with delight.

"It's all right, Mom," said Meredith with a smile. "Go back to sleep."

"*What!*" shrieked Dr. Samson.

"Come on, Fred. I'll explain everything." Dr. Fitzhugh put his arm around his bewildered friend and led him from the room.

CHAPTER THIRTY-SIX

Three Knocks and Two Letters

The next day, Meredith awoke refreshed in her own bed in her own room. How wonderful it was to be home! Later, she would see if Queen Esmerelda felt up to baking cookies with her. But first, there was something important she needed to do. She went to her desk and started to write a letter to Peter Porter. Then she stopped. She did not know whether he had made it back or not. She decided to send him a letter anyway.

> Dear Peter,
>
> I am back in Almira. Are you? If you are, I could use your help in setting Almira to rights. Remember those long talks we had in Rupert's dungeon about the value of representative government? Well, I am ready to give the dragons and humans of Deweydaire a chance to govern themselves.

She stopped, chewed her pencil—a bad habit—and thought a bit before continuing:

> Peter, I am sorry for the things I said to you at Nelda's. You probably didn't understand why I wouldn't go with you and Ben. I'm not sure I understand it, myself. You had come so far and

risked so much for me. All I know is that I had to follow my own path.

Just then, she heard a dog barking. That was strange. She hadn't seen any dogs at the palace since her return. She opened the door. To her great delight, there stood:

"Peter and Ferdie! I wasn't sure if I'd ever see you again. Peter, you've grown so tall!" She found herself looking up at him.

"Yes, I grew up fast in the real world," he quipped.

They hugged, while Ferdie got up on his hind legs to add his enthusiasm with his paws up on Meredith and his tail wagging happily. She did not stop him—just this once.

"Ferdie, how in the *world* did you get here?" Meredith said, ruffling his fur affectionately.

"That's a story only Ferdie can tell," said Peter, "although I know some of it. He's my dog now. I'm back at my old job as a palace messenger boy—part time. And you've got mail. It's a letter from Duke Ralph of Rhapsody Castle."

"Uncle Ralph!" cried Meredith, ripping open the envelope.

Greetings Meredith!

It is I, your Great-uncle Ralph. Welcome home! I've just arrived home, myself, from my genealogical expedition which has taken me to many strange and marvelous places. Boy, am I pooped! It was worth it, though. What did I learn? Things both important and unimportant. Maybe I will write a book about it all one day. What really matters is that I am still your uncle and I love you very much.

Now that I'm home, I'll be taking the throne back from Rupert. Was I mad when I found out what he had done to you. Positively *fuming*! I'm sending him over to you now to punish him as you see fit. I'll see you soon, after I've rested up.

Much love,
Uncle Ralph

PS: Don't let anyone tell you we dragons can't fly. I've been doing it for years! For we are not so much bound by physical barriers as by the limits of our imagination. As one of my 'traveling companions' once put it:

Be like the bird, who,
Halting in her flight
On limb so slight,
Feels it give way beneath her,
Yet sings,
Knowing she hath wings.

"I like that!" said Peter. "Seriously, Meredith, what *are* you going to do with Rupert? I know a pond where we can get a bucketful of frogs. He's terrified of them, you know."

"Is he?" Meredith looked uneasy. She did not relish frogs much, herself.

"Never mind the frogs, then," said Peter. "But, Meredith, you do have to punish him, after what he did to you."

"And to you!" said Meredith. "Don't worry, Peter. Rupert will have his day in court. He'll have a fair trial, just as soon as it can be arranged."

Just then there was another knock at the door.

"Who is it?" She couldn't make out the muffled response. She walked to the door and pulled it open. There stood a dragon wearing false glasses, bushy eyebrows, and a big nose.

Meredith was about to shut the door in his face when he pulled off his mask.

"Felix!" cried Meredith. "You joker! Come in, come in!"

"You are looking well, dear lady," said the jester, bowing low.

"Thank you. You, too, without that mask! Tell me, what brings you to Almira?"

"I was on my way here to discuss some business with Peter when I learned, to my great surprise and elation, that you had returned!"

"Felix has been trying to help our family get our farm back," explained Peter.

"Yes, I'm Rupert's number one advisor now. You might even say I run Rhapsody," said the jester "modestly."

"Or did," said Peter. "I've just heard Duke Ralph is back. That makes you the number two man now."

Felix's jaw dropped in surprise, but he quickly composed himself and flashed Meredith his toothy dragon grin. Meredith found it—and him—entrancing.

"Come, dear lady," he said, "don't keep me in suspense. Tell me everything that has befallen you. But perhaps I should be addressing you as Your Majesty." He bowed low.

"Not so fast, Felix. Yes, Esmerelda has declared me the new queen; but I'm thinking seriously about abdicating the throne—you know, giving it up—in favor of a democracy. We could hold an election to let the dragons and people vote for their own leaders. What do you think?"

"I think it's splendid—but risky," said Felix. "Your constituents may not vote for you, and Almira needs a strong leader, especially with the oat and potato famines we've been having lately."

"Famines!" cried Meredith.

"Don't worry; it's all under control," Felix reassured her hastily, "thanks to Peter's mother. She's discovered new crops that will grow better here than oats and potatoes ever did. She also has a way of getting people to try new foods. Why, her new stew with nine different grains and vegetables has been a big hit with dragons and humans alike. Even Rupert likes it—cold, of course."

"I've always wondered," said Peter, "why *do* you dragons eat everything cold?"

"That's simple," said Felix. "It's because we are already so full of hot air."

"Speak for yourself," Meredith retorted.

Felix flashed his toothy grin again. How could she have never noticed before how attractive he was?

"Come, Meredith," Felix said eagerly. "Shall we walk in the garden to discuss all this further?" He shot Peter a meaningful glance.

"Excuse me," Peter said, catching his hint, "I've got to go study my law books."

"Law books!" cried Meredith.

"You're studying law now? I don't believe it," Felix scoffed.

"And why not?" said Peter with indignation. "After all, if a court jester can become number one advisor to a prince, surely a poor farm boy can study law! Francis the Chancellor is helping me, in his spare time."

"Peter, that sounds wonderful!" cried Meredith. "I want to hear all about this later, for legal knowledge will be useful in our new government, one where everyone will have a say—dragons and humans alike. Oh! I have so many ideas! Do come back tomorrow, Peter, and bring your father with you."

"I'll come, but Dad is out on another mission. He's trying to recruit for your service those faithful rebel dragons who remained true to your Cause."

"I could always count on you and your father," said Meredith.

"And now you can count on me, too," said Felix. "Shall we take that walk in the garden now?" He offered her his scaly arm, and she took it. He seemed so confident and self-assured. She would have to get to know him better.

Just then, there was one last knock at the door.

"Come in," Meredith sang out happily. "Oh—it's you, Rupert." Her smile faded.

He was a sorry sight indeed, with his head bowed and his wrists chained to two of his own mean-looking guards.

"Hello cousin," he said, looking up hopefully. "I thought I'd never see you again. Heh heh." He sniffed the air appreciatively. "Say, do I smell just-baked oatmeal cookies? Mmm!"

Oh! How *could* he bring up cookies! As if he had done nothing wrong! He should be on his knees, sobbing and begging her for mercy!

"Rupert, is that all you can say? Not, 'I'm sorry for the terrible things I did?' ... No? ..." She would not let him spoil her day.

"Guards, take him away! We'll deal with Rupert another way— in court!"

Let us close the curtain now. For this ends our story, the story of a determined dragon, full of courage and hope, and of her daring friends who risked their all to help her regain her freedom. Farewell to Deweydaire, as dragons once again take to the air!

ACKNOWLEDGEMENTS

Christie heartily thanks: Lane Waldman for creating all of the wonderful, original illustrations found in this book and on the cover, Elana Seplow-Jolley of New Moon Editorial for her generous and apt developmental critique; David Kowalski for editing and being supportive in all the important ways; and Mark Pogodzinski and his NFB Publishing team for their exceptional efforts in helping Meredith to "fly."

The Voice of the Wooden Dragon was inspired by "Meredith," a wooden statue of a dragon created by Bill Loomis of Carbondale, Illinois. Christie first met Bill and saw the statue in progress in 1982. She completed her story, "Meredith," in the summer of 1983, after finishing her first year of law school at Southern Illinois University School of Law. She began to expand and revise the story in 1992. She is grateful to early readers: Jillian, Lane, and Eliza Waldman, Professor Henry S. Vyverberg of Southern Illinois University, Edith McIlveen and others in her church-based writing group, Mary Reed, Amy Mantell, Karen Zeilman, Kathy Davis, and her attentive early audience of children from the Rochester Area Homeschoolers Association. To all who have offered help and encouragement along the way, she is extremely grateful.

For background on St. George (treated in chapter 20), Christie found useful Christina Hole, chapter 2, "St. George of England," *Saints in Folklore*. New York: William Morrow, 1965. 17-32.

For background on Christian Jensen Loftuus (treated in chapter 32), Christie found useful: Knut Gjerset, *History of the Norwegian People*, vol 2 (of 2). New York: AMS Press, 1969 [1915]. 57-58; Halvdan Koht and Sigmund Skard, *Voice of Norway*. New York: Columbia University Press, 1944. 364-369; and "Norway's Sons of Liberty," *The Flyer*, May 2017. http:// www. sofnalaska.com/wp-co ntent/uploads/2017/05/ The_Flyer_2017_May.pdf.

ADDITIONAL CREDITS

- Collodi, Carlo [Carlo Lorenzini]. *The Adventures of Pinocchio: Story of a Puppet*. Translated by John Hooper and Anna Kraczyna. New York: Penguin, 2021. First published as "Le avventure di Pinocchio. Storia di un burattino," in *Il Giornale dei bambini*, 1881-1883.

- Drake, Milton, Al Hoffman, and Jerry Livingston. "Mairzy Doats." Miller Music Pub. Co., 1943.

- Fisher, W. A. "Going Home." 1922. An adaptation and arrangement of Anton Dvorak's Symphony No. 9 in E Minor, Op. 95, B. 178 (1893), subtitled and commonly known as the New World Symphony.

- Hanna, William, and Joseph Barbera, creators and directors. *The Jetsons* television series. Hoyt S. Curtin and Hoyt C. Curtin, music composers. First aired on September 23, 1962.

- Hugo, Victor. "Be Like the Bird." *Illustrated Poems for Children*. Illustrated by Krystyna Stasiak. New York: Checkerboard Press, 1989. 57. From "Dans l'eglise de," in *Oeuvres de Victor Hugo/Poésie/Victor Hugo [III], Les chants du crepuscule*. Bruxelles: Laurent, 1836.

- Key, Francis Scott. Lyrics to "The Star-Spangled Banner." First printed in Baltimore, 1812, as "Defense of Fort M'Henry."

- Kipling, Rudyard. "The Man Who Would Be King." *Rudyard Kipling: Stories and Poems*. Edited by Daniel Karlin. Oxford: Oxford University Press, 2015. First published in *The Phantom Rickshaw and Other Eerie Tales*. Allahabad, India: A. H. Wheeler, 1888.

- Lennon, John, and Paul McCartney. "Norwegian Wood." Recorded by The Beatles on *Rubber Soul*. Sony/ATV Music Publishing LLC, 1965.

- Yarrow, Peter. "Puff the Magic Dragon." 1962. From a poem by Leonard Lipton. 1959. First recorded by Peter, Paul, and Mary on *Moving*. Warner Brothers, 1962.

- *The Voice of the Wooden Dragon* is typeset in Lora (designed by Olga Karpushina and Alexei Vanyashin, Cyreal Foundry, Almaty, Kazakhstan), additionally with Cinzel Decorative (designed by Natanael Gama, NDiscover, a Digital Type Foundry, Lisbon, Portugal) on the cover and Koch-Antiqua Zier (a digitization of *Die Zierbuchstaben zur Koch-Antiqua*, designed by Rudolf Koch for the Klingspor Foundry, 1922-29, by Dieter Steffmann, Typographer-Mediengestaltung, Kreuztal, Germany) on the title pages.

Christie Waldman has wanted to be a writer ever since the second grade when she had a teacher who thought writing stories and plays was a worthwhile school activity. Christie's stories and poems have appeared in *Ember: A Journal of Luminous Things, Skipping Stones, and Westward Quarterly.* Although she grew up in Central Illinois, she has lived in Western New York since 1985, the year she graduated from Southern Illinois University School of Law. In 2018, her book, *Francis Bacon's Hidden Hand in Shakespeare's* The Merchant of Venice: *A Study of Law, Rhetoric, and Authorship,* was published (New York: Algora Publishing). She is a member of the Francis Bacon Society and a featured contributor at SirBacon.org. Her website is https://christinagwaldman.com.

Lane Waldman grew up in Rochester, New York and currently lives in Philadelphia, Pennsylvania. They graduated from Connecticut College. Aside from making art, they are also a writer of science fiction and fantasy; their stories have appeared in *Uncanny, Daily Science Fiction*, and *Capricious*, among other places.

Marcus A. Dragon is a stickler for factual accuracy. This is his first novel.

www.ingramcontent.com/pod-product-compliance
Lightning Source LLC
Chambersburg PA
CBHW071142260626
47162CB00003B/883